RESUSCITATION

NOLON KING

CJ LYONS

STERLING & STONE

RESUSCITATION

<h1 style="text-align:center">Chapter One</h1>

EASTFORK, NY
Friday, February 13th, 7:37 P.M.

SEVEN MEN DRESSED in black and wearing unmarked ballistic vests jostled in their seats as the dark Ford van rumbled through the night. Outside, a storm raged, the windshield wipers frantically sweeping away the snow, gusts of wind battering the vehicle, buffeting the passengers.

In the dimly lit rear, each man inspected his gear—checking sidearms, mics, and earpieces. Satisfied with their equipment, one after another they pulled on night vision goggles, confirming they were operational with a quick thumbs-up.

Their leader sat in the seat diagonally behind the driver. Andrew Mercer eyed each of his men in turn before opening a large Pelican case and removing law enforcement-issue Heckler & Koch MP5 submachine guns. The H&Ks hadn't been cheap or easy to come by, but with everything riding on tonight's success, they were worth the investment. He handed out the MP5s along with their 30-round magazines, finishing with a trio of flash-bang grenades for each of the team.

As his team inspected their new armaments, eyes gleaming like kids on Christmas morning, Mercer unholstered his own Glock 22 semiautomatic, checked the rounds of Speer gold dot ammunition, and slapped the magazine into place with a familiar click before racking the slide to place a live round in the chamber.

Satisfied that his men were ready, Mercer moved into the front passenger seat beside the driver, carefully placing the last MP5 alongside the van's central console.

"We're good to go," he told Connor, the driver.

Connor, eyes narrowed to see the highway through the relentless barrage of snow, gestured to an exit sign. "This it?"

Mercer frowned. At the snow, at the sign he could barely read through the fog, but mostly at the lack of enthusiasm in Connor's voice. His little brother was the whole reason tonight was happening—to make up for everything that had gone wrong in their lives, to pay back the man who'd stolen so much from them, to finally get what he and Connor deserved. A little appreciation of Mercer's hard work wasn't too much to ask for, was it?

"Take the exit and turn left," he replied. "Our road is another two miles after."

Connor veered onto the exit, the rear of the van shimmying as the tires fought for traction. As he slowed for the turn onto the county road, Mercer saw him glance at the rearview mirror and the dark clad, dangerous-looking figures hunched in the back, slapping magazines onto their new weapons with dark determination.

Enough of this shit, Mercer thought. Kid needed to get

his thinking straight before the action started. "Spit it out. What's eating at you?"

"Yeah, uh, I'm just thinking." Not Connor's strong suit, but Mercer didn't say anything—ever since Connor got out of the joint, he seemed even more hesitant than he used to be. As if a few years in prison had drained his will to take ownership of anything, much less his own damn life. Another reason for tonight—Mercer was certain that once they got what they came for, Connor would regain his spark, go back to the little brother Mercer missed so bad it felt like a part of him had vanished.

Connor continued, "Like, don't you think this is all overkill? For one guy, I mean. Plus, don't we have the element of surprise?" Connor looked at his older brother hopefully, as if he might agree and call the whole thing off.

"One guy—one guy who murdered our grandfather in cold blood." Mercer's voice dropped low and deadly, a rattlesnake spitting venom. "One guy holed up in a mansion fortress up in the mountains with what he stole. From us. One fuckin' guy. We're not taking any chances with this sonofabitch."

Connor nodded, his expression locked down tight, giving nothing away. "Sure, Andrew. You're the boss."

Mercer narrowed his gaze as he studied his little brother. "Hey, you know I've got your back, right? Think I'm gonna let you down?" He winced at the unspoken "again" floating between them. Not again. *Never* again. "No damn way. We're going in and taking back what's ours."

"No, no, I know that. I know that." Then he said the word Mercer had been waiting for. "Thanks. You could've taken off, didn't have to wait for me to get out. Thanks. For everything."

Mercer nodded, satisfied. He needed everyone on the

same page here. He'd spent years of his life tracking down Watts, their grandfather's killer. The man who had stolen the priceless Bitterroot Stars, rubies which were rightfully theirs. A man who was meant to be his father's best friend, who'd been Connor's godfather for chrissake. Tonight, the traitor was going to pay for fucking with the Mercer family.

As silence filled the front of the van, in the back, one of the crew, Mark Evans, an agile, small-framed man, toyed with a portable keypad that emitted annoying click-clacks.

"You gonna get us in clean this time, Marky Mark? Unlike that crapshoot job over in Cleveland?" a voice cut in. It was Leon, with a freshly shaved, blond crewcut and a perpetual scowl. "Tripped every damn sensor in the place."

"Jesus, you still going on about that shit? It was two years ago. And no, I didn't trip every sensor…one went off for about a millisecond, so fuck you."

"Ooohhh, did I trigger you?" Leon cooed before turning to the figure hunched next to him, a large man combing through the snaking mohawk centered on his shaven skull. "You get me, right, Brick? Got no time for fuckups, right?"

Brick, still combing, glared at the two men. Mercer always laughed at how the ugliest man he'd ever met was fanatical about maintaining his weird-ass haircut. "Knock it off, both of ya. Not the time for draggin' up ancient history."

"Yeah, shuddup, dickwipe," Mark chimed in.

Jonah Harper, a tall and imposing South African mercenary, checked his equipment with an almost obsessive attention. "I can tell you all one thing. The power'll be out in seconds. There'll be no mistakes from me," he stated, his tone leaving no room for doubt.

Across from him, Tyson Wallace rolled his eyes, a smirk playing on his lips. "There you go again, actin' like you're the only one who knows what he's doing. Just cuz you've got that sexy accent going on."

"Someone's gotta make up for the general lack of brains around here," Harper retorted, buttoning a pair of wire cutters into his chest pocket.

Leon chuckled, a dark, throaty sound. "Y'all can keep up chatting all night long. As long as I get to shoot something, I'm happy."

"Jesus, Leon," Connor called from the front, his voice strained. "We're not here to murder anyone."

"Speak for yourself," Leon muttered under his breath.

Mark glanced at Mercer in the front cabin, his face a mask of unease. "He's kidding, right? We're just here for the rubies."

Mercer glared—not just at Mark, but at each of the men in turn. "Stay focused and do your jobs. We get in, get what we came for, everyone goes home."

Tyson cracked his knuckles, the sound loud in the confined space. "But if someone gets in our way…"

"Then we do what needs to be done," Mercer finished, his tone leaving no room for doubt or hesitation.

They drove on silently, taking another turn onto a smaller, rural road which snaked up into the mountains. Connor had to slow on the slick, unsalted road, and after what seemed like an eternity, Mercer checked the map app on his phone and turned to his crew.

"Two klicks out."

The van fell into another heavy silence, each man left to his own thoughts. They drove around a bend in the road where a high stone wall and gates came into view. Beyond it, the unmistakable shape of the hulking three-story coal baron mansion waited.

Mercer gestured to a clearing just short of the walls. "This is it. Pull over here."

Connor killed the engine and lights as Mercer lowered a pair of night vision goggles and scanned the scene.

"Still can't see jack shit even with these," he muttered. He could tell the house was dark. No lights. He wished he'd had enough cash to spring for the fancy thermal NVGs, but he'd figured weapons took priority, so all they had was a cheap thermal imaging camera stolen from a fire station. They'd need to get closer to get inside the camera's range. He turned to his gang. "You all know what to do. Go, Bravo and Delta."

The rear door opened, and a rush of harsh, cold air, along with a flurry of snow, blew into the vehicle. Harper, aka Bravo, and Mark, Delta, jumped out into the shadows, donned their NVGs, and made a beeline for the wall.

From his perch in the front passenger seat, Mercer watched Harper crouch down while Evans climbed onto his back. Then Harper slowly stood up, giving his buddy the extra height they needed. Evans shimmied sideways onto the wall, slipped a pair of wire cutters out of a pocket, and snipped away at the razor wire which crowned the top of the wall.

Once clear, he hauled himself up and then leaned down to help Harper up, then they both jumped down inside the perimeter. They paused for a few seconds, then moved silently through the falling snow, keeping either side of the long drive toward the main building, the looming mansion that stood stoically in the darkness.

Mark located the alarm panel near the main entrance, began carefully unscrewing the protective casing, swung the panel door aside, and studied the maze of circuits inside. He knew the model and how to disable it, but he'd never performed such intricate work while fighting against driving wind and snow. Once Harper cut the power, the alarm would be out of action, but they couldn't risk some backup power randomly kicking in, bringing the alarm system back to life. So, it had to be disabled first.

He connected his portable keypad to the panel's input system and began entering default installer codes, hoping their target had neglected to change them.

No luck. The codes were rejected, but Mark didn't panic; he was prepared for this. He reached for his multi-meter and placed an insulated mat on the ground. Disconnecting the panel's power supply was delicate work, and one misstep could trigger the alarm he was trying to disable.

He identified the live wires with the multi-meter, his movements precise and controlled. Using wire cutters, he carefully severed the connections to the sensors and siren, then bridged specific circuits to create a false loop, making the system believe all sensors were in their neutral state. He also found and disabled the tamper circuits, ensuring no backup alarm would be triggered. Then the ex-con activated his radio and spoke into an earpiece that had been plugged into it.

"Delta to Bravo. Alarms down. Over."

"Roger that," came Harper's reply from his planned position near the house.

The South African had been recruited for this job by Mercer's ex-cell mate, Brick. Harper had located the electrical box on the wall of the house and crouched down in front of it, adjusting a small, red lens headlamp. Then he pried the box door open with a flathead screwdriver and scanned the complex wiring inside for a few moments before flipping the main breaker switch. There was a secret, secondary compartment where the backup battery resided. But it couldn't hide from Harper, not for long.

Using wire cutters, he severed the connection to the battery, ensuring it couldn't power the system.

He pressed his finger to his earpiece and spoke quietly into mic on his lapel, wired to the walkie-talkie on his belt. "Bravo to Alpha. Power and alarms are down. All clear to proceed. Out."

In the van, Brick set up a DragonMart DMJ-208 signal jammer with a range of up to 150 meters to block mobile and GPS signals. Mercer jumped out of the vehicle, jogged up to the gates, and pushed them open. He hesitated for a moment, shoulders hunched in anticipation of alarms that never came. Brick's man, Harper, had performed as promised.

Connor started the van, kept the lights off, and drove through the gates. Mercer climbed back into the passenger seat, and the vehicle crept up the drive. "Twelve minutes until the alarm company's response car arrives."

"You sure it's just a square badge, not the cops?" Connor asked, glancing at his brother.

"Watts is a fugitive. He wouldn't risk calling the cops. Besides, they'd be even slower, especially in this weather." The van stopped outside the historic mansion's entry. Mercer exited with the handheld thermal imaging camera and pointed it at the building.

"Let's see where you're hiding, Watts." He crunched through the thick snow along the front of the building until a heat signal displayed on his screen.

"Gotcha!" Mercer keyed his radio. "Target in second-floor front bedroom. Connor, Brick, on me." He slapped the camera into Brick's hand, gesturing to the remaining men with hand signals to circle around and enter from the other side. The figures soon disappeared into the blizzard.

Mercer flipped on his NVGs and strode to the front door, MP5 at the ready. Connor and Brick followed close behind. Mercer tapped the door with the butt of his rifle, then slammed his boot against the wood, crashing it open without resistance. The fancy electronic locks, now without power, had been rendered completely useless.

"Careful," Connor blurted, but Mercer was already stepping over the threshold.

He stopped abruptly once inside. "What the fuck?"

Pile upon piles of junk filled the foyer, reaching almost to the second floor. Bathtubs, bicycles, chairs, tables, shelves, old TVs, and appliances had all been thrown together, turning the interior into a literal dumping ground. Who knew what booby-traps could be hidden in the haphazard hoard that blocked passage to the staircase? Connor and Brick came alongside him, eyeing the flea market carnage.

"He's on the move," Brick muttered, tilting the angle of the display on the imaging camera to show Mercer. The man-shaped blob of heat seemed to ooze above them, headed toward the east wing of the house.

Static buzzed in Mercer's ear. "Sierra to Alpha. We're in the kitchen, but it's blocked. There's shit everywhere. Over."

Before Mercer had a chance to respond, the world turned white. An intense, bright glare frazzled his eyesight. He ripped off his NVGs and squinted, rifle raised toward where the blob that had to be Watts had last been.

A voice boomed out from above. "Stop! Don't move or you're a dead man, Andy Mercer!"

He froze. Gradually Watts came into focus, crouched next to a giant spotlight positioned halfway up the stairs. The old man held a shotgun aimed directly at Mercer's head.

Chapter Two

FRIDAY, February 13th, 5:58 P.M.

BLAKE HARROW ROLLED over in his bunk and opened his eyes to the digital clock. It read 5:58 p.m.

He waited until the alarm went off at six, then slammed the button to kill it. This routine of waking before the alarm happened every evening. A habit born years ago in basic training and, later, Ranger School.

The cabin's window revealed swirling snowfall as howling wind rattled the ancient glass panes. The temperature inside the rough-hewn log cabin had fallen several degrees since he'd gone to bed seven hours ago, but he wouldn't be here long enough to worry about it.

Another night, another dollar.

The thought was laced with satisfaction rather than contempt.

Truth was, he loved his job as an EMT. It'd allowed him to finally create a stabilizing rhythm, a foundation, as he slowly rebuilt his life, one day at a time. Or night. He worked the graveyard shift, eight p.m. to eight a.m., because that's how he liked it. He didn't have to see or speak to anyone when he was at the cabin, but he still got some social interaction with his colleagues at work.

Blake reached over, switched on the bedside lamp, and stood. Then he began to make up the bunk quickly and expertly, as if ready for inspection.

Making your bed as soon as you got up somehow fostered that sense of discipline and set a positive structure for the rest of the day. That's how Blake saw it anyhow, although no doubt younger souls, Gen Z or whoever, would laugh in his face.

He rolled out his exercise mat in the sparse yet immaculate room, in front of the double doors leading out to a small deck which usually held a commanding view of the lights of Eastfork down in the valley below. However, tonight the snowstorm obscured it. Sitting cross-legged on the mat, Blake took a deep breath and felt the cool air fill his lungs.

One, two, three, four.

He held the air in for another four seconds, then exhaled slowly before continuing the cycle. The rhythmic box breathing calmed his racing heart, a technique he had learned in therapy to manage his PTSD.

The whistling wind outside the windows ebbed, flowed, and began to echo the Afghanistan sandstorms that were etched permanently into his mind. His thoughts inevitably drifted to his comrades, his friends, lost to the IED that had ripped through them in a split second. Despite his best efforts, the familiar surge of anxiety chipped at his heartbeat, and he tutted, growing frustrated at himself.

You're losing concentration, Blake.

Their faces. He needed to remember their faces

because they got further away from him every day, and there was no way he was ever going to forget his brothers.

Never.

Before he realized it, he was on his feet, rummaging through his army-issue trunk. He found the photo, the only one he had of his squad. The image was slightly pixilated, printed from a digital phone many years ago. He rubbed his thumb along the edge and nodded to himself, feeling his heartbeat calm. Each of their faces told a story and brought back snippets of memory: a joke he had shared or that time he got his ass kicked at cards.

Private Miller.

Blake often replayed that short conversation with the young soldier, turning it over and over in his head. The kid had been mentally struggling with the whole shit-show. Who wasn't?

Blake himself had been close to the edge, even before the IED. Miller hadn't wanted to go out that morning, like he knew something bad was destined to happen. But good-ole Sarge that he was, and Blake had bucked him up, pushed him to join the convoy.

He could've given the kid a break, let him ride it out just that one patrol. Then Miller would've lived.

Blake exhaled.

They weren't all angels.

A few of his squad members had been hard work to get along with, but that didn't mean they had to die that way. None of them did. And for what? To just end up tossing the whole country back to the Taliban? That was one big-ass joke he would never forgive the government for.

Get on with it, soldier. Blake shook his head, pushing back against that first tear which would inevitably lead to uncontrolled sobbing, followed by pure rage, and most likely end with kicking the shit out of anything that would break.

Instead, Blake returned the photo, closed the trunk, and sat down on the exercise mat.

This time, he pumped through a more rigorous workout routine: fifty push-ups and fifty sit-ups, followed by a set of squats to really get the blood pumping through his veins. As the endorphins kicked in, Blake began to feel a lot better and more positive while his anger faded.

After showering and dressing for work, he headed to the kitchen. His motions ingrained with repetition, he started his coffee. While it brewed, he turned his attention to whisking two eggs into one cast iron pan, then butter-basting a small steak in another. When everything was ready, he plated and ate from a small wooden table at the center of the small kitchen. There was no TV in the cabin. It had given him migraines, and he'd come to the decision that it was probably the worse invention humanity ever created, with the useless spout of shit it fed into millions of living rooms. Good riddance to it.

When he had finished eating, Blake cleaned all the plates and pans and put them neatly back into place. Then he threw on his jacket, slipped his good luck charm—his grandfather's old Zippo—into place, grabbed his truck keys, and headed out into the billowing snow.

Windshield wipers at max speed, Blake squinted at the road ahead. The only other traffic he encountered was a single snowplow before he spotted the familiar darkened four-story building that marked the former Eastfork Medical Center. He grimaced at the sight. The only lights where the ER used to be now displayed a new sign: Medi-Corps Minor Care Center. The old neon emergency sign was as dead as the rest of this godforsaken town.

"Damn bean counters," Blake muttered.

He pulled his truck into the staff parking lot and hurried inside, through the main doors, glad to be out of the wild elements. Brushing snow from his jacket sleeves, Blake walked past a radiology suite that lay dark and empty.

The Computer Axial Tomography (CT) and Magnetic Resonance Imaging (MRI) scanning machines, once the pride of the hospital, had all long been sold off, leaving only a portable x-ray machine, too old to be worth anything. Beyond the old radiology department, plastic sheeting covered the corridors leading away from the former ER, now used as the Minor Care Center.

Blake swiped an ID card against a locked door's keypad and stepped into the patient waiting area, adorned with plastic chairs and corkboards displaying posters such as one with a smiling couple looking down at their sleeping toddler: "Got a cough? Sore throat? Ear ache? We're here for you!"

Among these hopeful positive messages were ominous warnings: *This facility cares for minor ailments only! Anyone experiencing a true emergency will be immediately transferred at your own expense to Potsdam Medical Center.*

At the registration desk, an exasperated bearded man with his hand wrapped in a bloody kitchen towel was facing off with Angie, the clerk, who patiently tried to calm him. "I'm sorry, sir. As I said, we can no longer accept your insurance at this center."

"Why the hell not?" the man replied, struggling to control his anger.

Blake grimaced in sympathy, both for the man, who was just trying to get the healthcare he'd already paid for with his insurance premiums, and Angie, who was forced to relentlessly spiel out the same lines to hopeful patients who simply needed help.

"We are now owned by MediCorps, so you need to talk to your care provider…"

Blake nodded to her as he walked past her desk. The door to one of the triage rooms was open, and Dr. Sara Porter, her brown shoulder-length hair draped over the shoulders of a white lab coat, was examining a woman's arm. Blake couldn't help his smile—out of Sara's sight of course. But this hour, the hour between the start of Blake's shift and the end of Sara's when the clinic closed at nine, was the best hour of his day.

A man, who Blake assumed was the woman's partner, sat alongside, looking stricken. "I told you to wait for me to salt the steps—"

The woman's arm was swollen and reddened above the wrist. When Sara gently palpated the area, the woman cried out in pain. Blake would place money on it being fractured. From Sara's frown, she agreed with his drive-by diagnosis. A few months ago, when this had been a functioning emergency department in a fully staffed medical center, treating a simple broken bone was easy. For the doctors, the staff, the patients, their families.

Now, thanks to MediCorps, it was like running an obstacle course in a hurricane with live ammo firing at them.

"I'm afraid it does appear to be broken," Sara told them. "We'll know for sure after the x-ray, but with the main hospital closed, we have no orthopedic surgeons here anymore. In fact, we have no surgeons at all. We don't have operating rooms or equipment either."

"Damnit," the man muttered. "How're you gonna fix her, then?"

"Let's get you some pain medicine and a splint, then we can discuss options once I take a look at the x-ray," Sara said reassuringly.

"What options? There's a storm out there, in case you hadn't noticed." He gestured toward the entrance doors with their chipper signs.

Blake grabbed an empty wheelchair and brought it into the room, nodding at the couple before giving Sara a pensive smile which she returned.

The man sighed and patted the woman's shoulder. "It'll be okay, Carol. It's gonna be okay." He watched as Blake gently helped her into the chair. Sara walked alongside him as he wheeled the patient into another part of the building's old ER section, where Sara beckoned to a passing physician's assistant.

"Nick, can you take Mrs. Wells to a treatment room and call the x-ray tech?" she asked. The PA dutifully took over from Blake and headed down the hallway through a set of double doors, the patient's partner trailing behind.

Blake and Sara stood alone. The moment drew out, making the usually confident Blake nervous, unsure of what to say. Then she turned to face him and he forgot how to speak altogether. Dammit, happened every time. Like he was a stupid teenager all over again.

She absent-mindedly brushed a strand of hair behind her ear. "Weather like this, I was hoping for a quiet night of playing cards, maybe some TikTok dances."

"Ah, cards, yes, I'm good with that, but not sure my dance moves are what they used to be," he replied, cursing himself with every stumbling word.

"Not a dancing man, then?"

Blake wondered where this was going. "I…never dance, honestly. Way too self-conscious for that," he admitted. May as well be honest.

"What about karaoke?" Sara probed.

He looked at her with a sideways glance and caught a

wry smile on her lips. She was definitely teasing him. "That's my worst nightmare...ever."

They both laughed as they approached the ambulance bay that housed the EMS offices.

"How were the roads? Looks pretty rough out there," she asked, more seriously.

"Coming down pretty heavy. Driving down the mountain, I only saw one road crew out."

"Snowplows are under a private contract now, just like everything."

"Still got us." He nodded toward the Eastfork Emergency Medical Services seal on the ambulance bay doors.

Sara frowned. "You didn't hear? They're going to turn the ambulance service over to Potsdam. It's like the whole town's preparing to declare bankruptcy or something."

Blake stopped short. "What? They can't—that'll mean response times of an hour or more. Our patients are underserved as it is. They really don't deserve this."

"I love how you're more worried about your patients than the fact that it means you'll lose your job."

Blake rubbed his cleanly shaved chin as he absorbed the consequences of her words. Life was going to change. Jobs were going to be lost. "What about you? Surely, they can't close the ER?"

"Minor care center," she corrected. "Word is, once the government funding runs out, MediCorps is shutting us down like the rest of the hospital. Stripping us naked and selling off the parts."

He shook his head, lost in thought, surprised by how much the idea of never seeing her again upset him. Wherever his thoughts were going, he needed to secure that shit. He was no good for anybody, not with his damaged psyche, and there was no way he could risk hurting her if the PTSD got out of control again. She was a good doctor and could take her skills anywhere. She would help people wherever she ended up.

She had a future—and it wasn't with Blake.

"What am I gonna do?" She shrugged. "I've no idea, but things always work out, somehow. Don't they?"

Blake was about to say he wasn't too sure about that when Alyssa, the paramedic he partnered with, emerged from the EMS dispatch office. She tied her curly Afro back into a bun, then threw on a jacket over her dark green uniform.

He'd lucked out getting a partner like Alyssa. He admired her dedication, taking the graveyard shift while juggling college classes with work. She was the definition of driven, saving up to attend physician assistant school, even convincing Blake to study in order to someday upgrade from an EMT-A to paramedic himself. That was Alyssa, always with a plan. Which is why, even though she was fifteen years younger than he was, he didn't mind that she was his boss.

"Hey, guys, good timing," she said when she spotted them. "We gotta go. Sara's favorite frequent flyer needs transport to Potsdam."

Both Blake and Sara smiled. Thomas was one of their regulars, an elderly gentleman who had been part of the routine at the Medical Center—when the Medical Center had still existed—for so long that he felt like part of the family. Along with his chronic conditions, the shadow of prostate cancer was ever threatening to end his life, but Thomas always had a smile and a good story to cheer up everyone he met.

"Is it his kidneys or diabetes?" Blake asked. The renal failure that Thomas's severe diabetes had caused was a sideshow, or "shit-show" as he called it, to his cancer. He always joked he was taking bets on which would kill him first.

Sara said, "I'll bet he forgot his insulin. Last time he came in, I won the pool with a blood sugar of 468."

"Nah." Blake shook his head. "Thomas isn't one to make the same mistake twice. I'll go for kidneys."

Sara turned to Blake and raised an eyebrow. "Usual bet?"

"Giant bag of Peanut M&M's? Sure thing," Blake replied with a grin.

Alyssa shook her head with a knowing smile that said "get a room, already" and held up the ambulance keys. "C'mon, partner, time to roll out and rock."

Chapter Three

Newark, NJ
  Eight years ago…

It seemed the long, hot summer evening would never end. Andrew Mercer and his brother, Connor, strolled along the avenue, heading to their house in Springfield-Belmont. They passed shuttered storefronts with boarded windows plastered with graffiti. Vacant lots filled with overgrown weeds and derelict buildings had replaced what was once a bustling neighborhood.

Newark was meant to be the promised land for the Mercer family. When Andrew was eight and Connor four, Jamie, their father, had fled the dead-end mining jobs back in Montana after their grandfather had been killed by their neighbor and Jamie's best friend, John Watts.

With Watts went the rubies their grandfather had smuggled out of the Bitterroot Star mine—and with the rubies went any chance Mercer and Connor had for a future.

"We really gonna do this?" Connor asked as they passed two girls sitting on a stoop, slurping Icees.

"No choice," Mercer told him, shifting his empty gym bag. "We're down to a few hundred bucks, and Dad's—"

"Dad," Connor finished with a sigh. "I dunno, maybe we could go legit. I heard they're hiring at—"

"Fuck legit." Mercer wheeled on his brother. "It's all on us, now. We gotta take back what's ours. That shit Watts murdered Grandpa, took the rubies. Our rubies." Fighting the urge to shake sense into his brother, he instead took out a cigarette from his pack and lit it. Inhaled, refocused. "Yeah, we do the job. Gives us cash flow. Then we can put things in place to go after Watts. Once we find him, we'll need decent shooters, equipment. Maybe a few more guys. None of that comes cheap."

They continued past a liquor store and down a block. Mercer tossed the cigarette butt as they turned onto their street, past a collection of older multi-family homes, husked-out derelicts, and an abandoned Baptist church.

The Mercer family home was one of a row of identical pre-war brownstones. When they entered, the stench of urine mixed with cheap whiskey hit their nostrils. Jamie lay slumped at the kitchen table, a half-empty bottle within easy reach.

"What's goin' on, Dad?" Mercer asked loudly, dumping his sports bag on the floor.

Jamie spasmed into life and jerked his head up, eyes rolling, his bushy, black hair tussled from sleep, his once-athletic frame now thinner, scragglier. He rubbed his gray stubble and grunted before launching into a coughing fit.

"You gonna eat something? We got some leftover pizza," Connor offered.

Their dad waved a hand violently, continuing to cough. Once the fit had passed, he reached for the bottle and poured a generous serving into a nearby glass. Jamie knocked back his drink in one swift motion, grimacing as it burned down his throat. He reached for his cigarettes and lighter.

Mercer looked down at this father. The once-leader of the family, who'd kept the money coming in from numerous illegal activities, was now a shell of a man.

Growing up, the boys learned to steal, pickpocket, a dozen different rackets—their dad taught them everything he knew. The boys could only pray that they'd be able to please him with the loot they brought home. Otherwise, there'd be an inevitable mood switch that would end with a slap.

But Mercer had grown to respect the fear their father instilled, that volatile change of mood at the snap of a finger, his resolve and single-minded pursuit in the art of obtaining money by any means possible. Except for a "regular" job, of course. Their mother, Emily, was long gone, years before Jamie had trucked them across the country from Montana. So, despite their father's harsh demeanor, Mercer placed his old man on a pedestal.

He and Connor had a running argument. Mercer was certain that when he was eight and cut his arm on a jagged piece of metal in the front yard, his father had left work, dropped everything, rushed him to the hospital.

Connor said no, it was their neighbor, John Watts, who had taken Mercer while their dad played cards and drank whiskey.

"But I remember," Connor would say.

"You're wrong. Dad definitely took me," Mercer insisted. Then he'd roll up his sleeve, the long scar across his forearm his final rebuttal, and Connor'd shut up. Nice thing about being the big brother, he always got the last word.

Now Mercer watched his dad pouring another drink and knew it was Connor who held the truth about that day. And today, it was time for Mercer had to face that truth, step up, otherwise they were finished. It was all up to him.

"That goddamn fucking Watts!" Jamie screeched, hammering a fist on the table. Neither son startled—they were used to his rants. He pointed a finger at Mercer. "You better get him, ya hear? You get him!"

"We'll get him, Dad. We'll get him. Don't worry," Mercer assured him, looking directly at Connor.

Those rubies, rubies their grandfather died for, were supposed to have been their chance at a better life. Mercer imagined John Watts living it up, spending what should've been theirs, laughing at their misfortune.

The injustice of it all burned in Mercer's gut, fueling a rage he'd never felt before. He'd find a way to set things right, to reclaim what belonged to his family. No matter what it took, he silently vowed, John Watts would rue the day he double-crossed the Mercers.

But right now, they needed funds. Serious funds. And that meant doing the jewelry store across the river in New York. They'd been casing it all month. It was a big job. The biggest they had ever attempted, but the payoff was going to set them up on the road to finding Watts and the Bitterroot Star rubies.

~

EARLY THE NEXT MORNING, he and Connor waited in their stolen sedan, plated especially for the job. When the jewelry store owner, an elderly woman, opened up, they rushed in after her, fully masked, and slammed the door behind them.

"Down! Get on the ground!" Mercer barked, brandishing his pistol and pointing it squarely at the woman's forehead. She froze in shock, her eyes darting between the gun and the two men.

"Please! I—I don't want any trouble!" she stammered, her voice quaking with fear.

"No talking, just do what I say! Open the goddamn cabinets." Mercer gestured with his gun.

Connor's gaze darted from the woman to his brother, needing both hands to hold his pistol steady.

The woman's hands moved slowly, shaking as she fumbled with the keys at her waist.

"Keep eyes on her," Mercer ordered Connor. Mercer slipped his own pistol into his belt and pulled out the large sports bag. With a swift motion, he reached inside the open case and grabbed fistfuls of the jewelry, throwing it all into the bag.

"More! Keep going, open the others," he urged her, his voice laced with threat.

The woman moved as fast as she could, unlocking cases. There was a momentary, tense silence punctuated only by rapid breaths and the sound of gold, stones, and other precious jewels clunking into the bag.

"That'll do, right? Let's get outta here." Connor stepped forward from where he'd been keeping an eye on the door.

"In a sec. Where's the good stuff?" Mercer demanded. "You got a safe back there?"

She dropped to her knees, making Mercer wonder if she had some kind of floor safe. Shit, no, she was reaching for something else.

"Stop! Shoot her, Connor!" Mercer shouted, fumbling his own gun free with one hand, unwilling to drop the bag with the jewelry.

But Connor froze. He shook his head as if he hadn't understood Mercer's words.

"Shoot the bitch!" Mercer screamed.

In one desperate, final act of defiance, the woman pressed her palm against the alarm button. A blaring blast erupted through the store.

Pistol finally in his grip, Mercer aimed at the back of her head, anger surging through him.

Connor stopped him. "Let's go!"

Mercer bared his teeth, his face contorted. "Fuck!"

They turned, scrambled to open the door, and ran to the car.

Almost made it, too.

Chapter Four

Friday, February 13th, 8:04 P.M.

Steering with one hand, Blake used his other to stab at the ambulance's radio controls for the fifth time. Only a crackling hiss came back in response.

"Dammit. I thought Wayne said this thing was fixed already," he muttered. He slammed the console with his palm before giving up.

"Now he gets to blame it on your physical abuse of corporate equipment, and they'll take it out of your paycheck," Alyssa quipped.

Blake smiled despite his growing frustration. "All my check will buy 'em is a toy walkie-talkie from the dollar store."

"Let me." She leaned forward, turned the radio off, then ever so gently, tapped it back on, giving the volume a slight nudge, re-setting the frequency just so, and then clicking the button. An energetic squawk filled the cab.

"Just needed a woman's touch," she said with a smirk.

"And you know what that means? She who wields the power of the radio—"

"No, please, no!" Blake said with mock terror.

"Wields the power of the muuuu-ssak!"

She produced her cellphone. A synth-pop track kicked in, booming through the cabin.

"Don't suppose you have some mellow sixties rock loaded on that thing?"

"Afraid not, old man," she shouted as she snapped her fingers and wiggled in the seat to the tune.

Blake shook his head in mock disgust. "This should be banned!"

"Oh, is this in your future-retro-imaginary society of guitar-based music and long hair?"

"Yes, absolutely. When I'm king, this will be banned, and we will revert forever back to the sixties."

"What do you know about the sixties, you weren't even born then!" Alyssa tilted her head as she contemplated this strange new world of Blake's. "So, in this nostalgic utopia, do we get cell phones, computers, internet?"

"Absolutely not. We get rid of it all. Re-install the land-lines and bring back the fax machine."

"And telegrams?"

Blake laughed. "Do you even know what that is?"

"Of course! I've seen old movies," she retorted.

"Yeah? Like what?"

"You know, *Casablanca*, that Kane one."

"*Citizen Kane*? Yeah, Orson Welles. Classic. I love the old movies. Especially the black and white ones," Blake said with a sigh.

"Oh my god, you look like forty-ish, but you have the mind of a seventy-something old geezer."

Blake couldn't help but laugh at that. "Hey, less of the 'geezer' talk, please. I'm thirty-nine, for your information.

But I still love the old stuff. Guess because my mom and I lived with Mom's parents." He smiled, remembering long summer nights when Pap-pap, a Vietnam vet turned dairy farmer, would strum his guitar and Nana sang. "Whatever, those days, their days, seem just…easier."

"Ah, yes, the good-ole olden-golden daysers," Alyssa said, rolling her eyes in mock jest.

"What's so good about nowadays? Just look at this place," he asked, gesturing at the main street of Eastfork as they drove. Signs declaring bankruptcy or going out of business sales were posted on almost every door and window.

"Seems like more places have shut since we were last here, right?" Alyssa leaned against the passenger window. The ambulance passed the old police station, now also boarded up. The mood in the cabin instantly changed.

"So goddamn sad," was all Blake could mutter in response to the bleak sight.

"And wrong. Where's our so-called government when you need it?" Alyssa added.

Blake's jaw stiffened. "Lining their own pockets and interests is what they're doing. Propping up the big corporations while throwing mom and pop businesses straight at the wall, just like during Covid."

He turned onto a residential street and pulled up outside a brick housing project, switching off the engine. "You got his key?"

"Yep," Alyssa replied, opening the lock box below the dash. Many of their "regulars" left spare keys with the ambulance service so they wouldn't need to call the fire guys to come knock down their doors if they were incapacitated. Saved time and money—the wait on the fire department was sometimes even longer than the wait for the cops, since the FD was all volunteer and guys had to drive in from home.

They went into the rear cabin of the truck, then grabbed their medical bags and the transfer chair. Thomas's building had no elevator, but he wasn't a big man, and carrying him down the three flights of stairs in the chair would be easier than wrestling the gurney.

"Ready?" Alyssa asked, bracing one hand on the ambulance's rear door. Blake nodded and she shoved it open. They stepped down into the howling wind and swirling snow. Heads bowed, they trudged up the snow-covered steps into the apartment building's lobby and headed up the steps to the third floor.

At Thomas's door, Alyssa knocked. No answer. Blake unlocked the door.

A pungent smell greeted them as they entered the cluttered apartment that had become a memorial to Thomas's late wife, Rose, whose photograph was centered on the pony wall that separated the tiny foyer from the kitchen and dining area. Other smaller photo frames displayed her through the decades, including one of their wedding many years before.

"Thomas?"

In the far corner, across from the small dining table in what passed for a living room but barely had space for a TV stand and coffee table, they found Thomas slumped in his worn recliner, his face a ghastly blue-gray color, sweating and barely conscious.

Prescription bottles were piled on an end table, and to one side of the recliner stood a cane, which Blake had never seen Thomas actually use. He was a proud man—one of the reasons why, when he called, they always knew it was serious. Thomas would never waste their time, not like some of their frequent flyers who really were just lonely and wanted company.

"Thomas, we're here," Blake assured him. The old man was almost totally blind, and Blake didn't want to startle him. He was rewarded by the old man's eyes flickering open, focusing as best they could on Blake.

He and Alyssa went into a familiar routine, one which they had performed on many previous visits.

While Alyssa listened to his heart and lungs, Blake checked Thomas's vitals and attached the chest leads and hooked Thomas up to the monitor. "Now I'm going to check your pulse oximetry." He clipped the pulse ox over Thomas's forefinger. "Heart rate 122, sats 92," he told Alyssa as he placed an oxygen mask over Thomas's face.

She nodded, removed her stethoscope. "Thomas, we're going to send an EKG to the hospital while I check your blood sugar."

Blake knew her words were as much for him as for Thomas. As they shifted position, Blake worked the monitor to record and send the EKG while Alyssa slid the glucometer from a pocket of her bag.

"Let's sit you up, Thomas." She helped the old man up. His color was better with the oxygen and he was more awake now. She swiped an alcohol pad over his finger tip. "A little prick."

"Never been called that before," Thomas said, his voice muffled by the oxygen mask.

Blake could tell he was trying to make light of the whole thing, but he still didn't look good. Not the Thomas Blake had come to care for.

"I would never be so rude," she replied. The tiny needle released a droplet of blood. Alyssa pressed the test strip to collect the blood and waited for the result. The glucometer beeped three times—a warning that the measurement was out of normal limits.

"Thirty-eight." Alyssa opened their med kit and grabbed the glucagon, deftly drawing it up into a syringe. "Okay, we can work with that. Blake, see if there's any juice in his fridge. If not, we'll start an IV here instead of waiting until we're in the rig. And check his insulin supply."

"You're gonna be just fine, Thomas," Blake said as he moved to the kitchen.

"You know the drill, Thomas," Alyssa said, holding up the syringe. "Where do you want it? Thigh, butt, or arm? You're so damn bony, it's gonna hurt wherever I give it."

In answer, he tugged at his shirt, trying to extract his arm but getting tangled in the oxygen tubing. Alyssa helped him open his shirt far enough that she could reach his deltoid muscle. He made a small groan when she injected the medicine.

Alyssa tossed the sharps in the disposal bin, then circled her fingers around his wrist, feeling his pulse. She could've just have easily read his heart rate from the monitor, but Blake knew she preferred the human touch. She always said she could tell a lot from how a patient's pulse felt, more than just counting their heart beat. "Better, already much better."

Blake pressed a glass of OJ into Thomas's hand and showed Alyssa his insulin doses, arrayed in two trays, one for evening, one for morning. Diabetes had ravaged Thomas's eyesight; he wasn't totally blind but the tiny numbers on insulin needles were too much for him to read, so he relied on the county health worker to measure out his dosages for the days between dialysis. Blake tapped the morning tray—there were two missing syringes.

"My fault," Thomas muttered, pushing aside the oxygen to sip at the OJ.

"Grabbed a morning syringe with the higher dose, instead of your evening one?" Alyssa's tone was gentle. "Honest mistake. I'm glad you called us when you did." She glanced at the monitor and took the oxygen off. "Drink."

As he obeyed, downing the OJ, she glanced around the apartment. "You know, Thomas, I think this place needs a serious makeover. It's starting to look like a set from a B-rated horror movie."

Thomas chuckled.

Almost back to normal, Blake thought. Almost.

"Horror movie? More like a classic! Every item here tells a story. Like that old lamp," Thomas said, gesturing to a tarnished piece that had seen better days. "That's from when we first got married."

"When was that again?" Alyssa asked. She was testing his orientation and memory, but doing it in a much nicer way than asking who the president was and the day of the week.

"July 1st, 1973. A sweltering day in Manhattan. At the reception, the AC was down. Fans blowing every which way, but they didn't help. Rose was so happy, though." His smile was laced with regret, and Alyssa touched his shoulder with quiet sympathy. "And all I cared about was that I had her."

"She was a beautiful woman," Blake offered, glancing at one of the many photographs.

"She was, she was," Thomas said quietly.

"Hey, you two stop. I'll be sobbing all the way back to the ER, the way you're carrying on," Alyssa interjected.

"Do I have to go?" Thomas asked. "I'm feeling better."

"That glucagon's gonna wear off, and you know with

your kidneys, you don't respond as well when your sugar gets out of whack," she reminded him. "Besides, don't you need to go to Potsdam for dialysis anyway? When's your appointment?"

That's what had been nagging at Blake as he'd looked through Thomas's fridge. The calendar on the front of the freezer door. He shot a look at Alyssa, and she waved for him to go on—they tried to only have one person asking questions so patients didn't get overwhelmed or confused about who they should be answering.

"Thomas," he asked in a gentle tone, "weren't you scheduled for dialysis today?" Dialysis days meant he'd need a lower dose of insulin than usual—something the clinic took care of before bringing him home. Or should have.

Thomas caught Blake's eye and nodded slowly. "They called, said cuz of the storm they had to cancel."

Alyssa and Blake exchanged glances. "Okay, new plan," Alyssa said. "Let me grab a quick I-stat, make sure your potassium isn't sky high." Blake moved to get the testing equipment for her. "Your EKG isn't showing any peaked T-waves, and Dr. Sara would've called if she saw anything worrisome, so—"

"If it's okay, I can stay here?" Thomas asked hopefully.

Blake knew how much he hated being away from his home and Rose's memories, even if just for a night. He also knew that even more than missing his home and routine, Thomas was frightened of dying surrounded by strangers in a strange place.

Deep down inside, despite the cold, hard fact that he could never risk the unpredictability and emotional gamble that came with starting a relationship, Blake realized he shared Thomas's fear: that he was doomed to live and die alone.

Chapter Five

FIVE DAYS AGO...

MERCER INHALED DEEPLY, savoring the crisp wintery air. After years of confinement, even the most mundane sensations felt like a luxury. He stood in a parking lot outside a nondescript bar on the outskirts of Newark, watching as Brick parked his car, a well-maintained old Charger. Brick exited the car, one hand fingering his freshly styled mohawk as he strolled to join Mercer.

"Gang's on their way," he said.

Mercer nodded approvingly. His old cellmate had proven himself a valuable ally inside and outside the prison walls. Those connections of Brick's were going to be crucial for what lay ahead.

They entered. It was early enough in the day that they were the only customers other than a single, wobbling drunk perched at the bar. Mercer led Brick to a large booth in the farthest corner.

A few minutes later, the first of Brick's crew arrived, a guy called Leon with shaven blond hair and an imposing frame that towered over them both. He gave Mercer a curt nod of appraisal before joining them.

"Good to see you, man," Brick greeted him. To Mercer, he said, "Leon is ex-Marine, handy in a fight."

After a few minutes, another man entered the bar with a duffel bag slung over his shoulder.

"Reporting for duty," the man quipped with a South African accent. He slapped palms with Leon. "How're you doing, dick job?"

"Mighty fine, asswipe."

Brick introduced the South African. "This is Harper. Handy with electrical issues."

"As well as weapons and any close combat situations," Harper added.

Behind him entered a squirrelly young man, bouncing on his toes. "And least as well as last, is my technowiz, Marky Mark Evans," Brick said.

The kid flinched. "Hey, I'm not last. Where's Tyson?"

"Right here." Tyson wheeled from the bar stool, suddenly very much sober. Smart, Mercer thought. Arriving early, checking the place. The Afro-Caribbean man exuded an air of quiet competence that Mercer found very reassuring.

With the team assembled, Mercer felt a surge of anticipation. These men were professionals, each bringing unique skills to the table. But there was still one piece missing: Connor.

Mercer threw down a gym bag filled with the last of his stashed cash. "The agreed upfront payment and expenses. We'll be staging out of a hick town in upstate New York, Eastfork. Plan for minimum of three days—final recon and the job. So, we'll need to find a place there where we can fly under the radar."

Brick nodded, a wolfish grin spreading across his face as he opened the bag and began divvying up the cash. "Already on it, boss. I'll text you the address of the place I rented."

"We'll go over final plans tomorrow. Today, I'm headed out to pick up my brother." Mercer checked his watch.

"Free at last, free at last!" Brick pumped his fist in the air, almost more excited than Mercer was that Connor was finally getting out.

"We'll spend the night in Albany, meet you guys in Eastfork tomorrow." Mercer stood, put his jacket on. "One thing before I go," he said, his tone grave. "I'm the boss when it comes to this operation. Is that understood?"

The crew sitting around in the booth all nodded.

"Goes without sayin'," Brick muttered. "You payin' the bills."

"Just want to be clear on that." He looked around at each of the crew in turn. "Next round's on me, and I'll see you tomorrow."

Mercer ordered the drinks, then left the bar and began the drive up to Shawangunk Correctional Facility.

An hour later, he leaned against his car, anxiously watching the prison gates. A smile broke across his face as he spotted a familiar figure emerging from the building. Looking thinner and more fragile than Mercer remembered, Connor stepped into the sunlight, squinting as he scanned the parking lot.

Mercer pushed himself off the car and strode forward, arms outstretched. "Hey, bro!"

The brothers hugged, years of separation melting away instantly. Mercer felt Connor's shoulders shake and heard a muffled sob against his chest.

Mercer quickly pulled back. "Hey, c'mon, don't break on me, man. I've got plans, little brother. Big plans," he said, attempting to keep the tone light.

As they drove away from the prison, Mercer filled Connor in. "Brick's on board and brought in some solid guys. We're all set. Now all we gotta do is track down Watts. I want to make sure he's home when we hit the place, see the look on his face—"

"I thought we were just gonna take the rubies. We're not gonna kill—"

"Yeah, of course we are. The bastard stole our future. It's his turn to pay."

"Yeah, but I just didn't think we'd—"

"Leave the thinking to me. We'll get what's ours, deal with Watts, and get across the border into Canada. I've got cash stashed. Enough so we'll be okay until we fence those rubies." Mercer glanced over, noticing the apprehension on Connor's face. "This is our chance. Set things right, take back what's ours."

"I don't know. It sounds risky. We just got out…"

Mercer's grip tightened on the steering wheel. "I know you're worried, bro, but trust me. We do this job, we're set for life. No more worries, no scraping around, no more looking over our shoulders." He softened his tone. "I need you with me on this, bro. We're family. We stick together, right?"

Connor nodded slowly, a faint smile touching his lips. "Yeah. Of course, Andrew."

Connor was the only person alive who called Mercer "Andrew." The thought made him a little sad to think they were the only two Mercers left.

Mercer gripped the wheel, eyes fixed on the snow-dusted road ahead as they drove north. The van's heater whirred softly, fending off the chill inside. Connor gazed out the window at the passing landscape, lost in thought.

The silence between them grew heavy, punctuated only by the hum of the engine and the fan heater. Thankfully, the sign for the cheap motel Mercer had booked for the night appeared.

The next afternoon, as they approached Eastfork, the wind whipped up, a new storm moving in from the west. Mercer slowed the car, peering through the windshield at the nearly deserted streets. The town seemed even more desolate than when he'd come here to do recon two weeks ago—shuttered storefronts, faded signs, and an air of neglect.

It was too soon to meet the guys, so Mercer stopped at the diner on the main drag. They ordered a couple of burgers and ate in silence before replacing their sodas with coffee.

Mercer stirred his absentmindedly, the spoon clinking against the ceramic mug. The diner buzzed with low conversations and the clatter of dishes.

Connor sat across from him, scanning the restaurant. "So, you reckon he's around here somewhere?" he asked, his voice low. "Watts?"

"Can't hide from the internet," he said. "Found him in the property tax records. Came up here myself to check it out the week after I got out. Place seemed deserted." Except for the fancy security system, that was. But he didn't want to dump too much on Connor all at once. Kid seemed more than a bit skittish. The joint could do that to a person.

Connor seemed relieved by Mercer's report. "Deserted? Maybe that's a good thing. Hit it while he's gone, let him be the one wondering what the hell just happened, ya know? It'd be kinda a form of torture, him coming home to find the rubies long gone."

"Yeah, but then we'd be the ones looking over our shoulders rest of our life. I don't want to live like that, do you?"

Connor's gaze dropped as if his empty coffee cup was more interesting than Mercer's words. "No. Guess not."

"Exactly. It's settled. Watts has to die."

Chapter Six

Forward Operating Base (FOB) Lagman,
   Zabul Province, Afghanistan.
   August 9, 2007

Sergeant Blake Harrow zipped his tactical vest, fingers running over the familiar contours of the gear he'd worn countless times since arriving in hell.

There was no other term for it.

American troops were losing limbs from IED attacks every other day on average, not to mention the countless, endless deaths.

Under the pre-dawn darkness that cloaked the army base, a soft murmur vibrated through the air: the soldiers of the 4th Brigade Combat Team, 82nd Airborne Division, Task Force Fury, preparing for battle. They moved purposefully, their boots crunching on the gravel paths between rows of dun-colored tents and Hesco barriers. The scent of diesel and dust hung in the air, mingling with the aroma of coffee wafting from the mess hall.

Engines from the trucks assigned to the morning patrols rumbled to life as mechanics performed last-minute checks. Blake caught snatches of conversation—gruff orders, idle banter, and the occasional laugh—as soldiers inspected their gear and psyched themselves for another day in hostile territory.

Nearby, a convoy of sand-camo RG-31 trucks lined up in formation, their armored bodies gleaming in the growing dawn light. Soldiers loaded supplies of ammo crates, med kits, and water cans into the vehicles—everything they'd need for an extended patrol. Blake's team was among them, stowing gear. He joined in, helping to finish the work quicker.

"No MRAPs?" he asked the corporal supervising the patrol vehicles.

"Not today, sorry."

Blake wasn't surprised, but he wasn't happy either. He approached Lieutenant Garcia, a seasoned officer who exuded a calm confidence and aura of professionalism. In other words, an officer who might—just might—not get Blake's men killed. "Good morning, Lieutenant Garcia."

"Sergeant Harrow. Ready for another fine day in paradise?"

"I thought we were going out in the MRAPs?" he asked Garcia. The Mine-Resistant Ambush Protected vehicles were the promised new answer to the scourge of IEDs, explicitly designed to withstand improvised explosive device attacks and ambushes.

"The new arrivals didn't pass inspection. Need their air filters upgraded to deal with the dust." The Lieutenant shrugged, a small movement that revealed his fatigue. "Guess they must've thought 'road ready' meant cruising some highway stateside."

"Yeah. Not like lives are on the line or anything," Blake muttered. "Thanks, LT."

He turned toward a sudden burst of laughter. A cluster of soldiers gathered around Sergeant O'Leary, leader of the other squad they'd be patrolling with. Must've been some joke, since everyone around him was brushing away tears from laughing too hard, even as they checked their equipment.

Blake wished he could be funny like that, but even though he'd never been married or had a kid, the only jokes he knew were "dad" jokes he'd learned from his grandfather. They made his guys groan and roll their eyes, not laugh.

Continuing toward his squad's vehicles, Blake noticed Private Miller, the youngest and newest man on Blake's squad, looking visibly upset. Blake followed him to Miller's quarters. He stepped inside, finding Miller seated on the edge of his cot, head in his hands.

"Miller?" Blake called out softly, approaching the distraught soldier. "What's going on?"

The kid lifted his head, grim-faced. He swiped at his eyes, but his tears didn't come from any gut-splitting joke, Blake was sure. "Sarge, I…I can't do this anymore," he choked out. "I just want to go home."

Blake sat down beside Miller. He remembered the raw fear and desperation he'd felt during his own early days in-country, which still morphed into the occasional anxiety attack. "You're not alone in that feeling."

They sat in silence, Blake not pressing the young soldier despite the fact that it was almost time to move out.

Finally, Miller spoke again, his words directed down at his boots. "It's just…" He paused, swallowing hard. "When Ellison got hit by the IED and didn't make it… We were friends, came through basic together…"

Blake instinctively placed a hand on Miller's shoulder, giving it a reassuring squeeze. He hadn't realized Miller and Ellison had been close friends. He wondered what slick words O'Leary would have to make things better, get Miller to laugh or at least smile.

Whatever words could perform that kind of magic, Blake didn't have them at his disposal.

"I'm sorry to hear that. Losing a friend is never going to be easy. It's..." The words sounded hollow, clichéd. Blake changed tactics. "Little while ago, I lost a friend. Carl, Carl Bukoski. Our squad was doing house searches. One of the locals, family man, acted like he had some intel to share, so we got too close and...Carl got killed."

Miller glanced up, eyes reddened but no more tears. "Sorry, Sarge. That sucks."

Blake blew out his breath. "Yeah. It does. It really, really does. And it hurts like hell." He tapped his fist against his thigh. "But you can't let it break you, Miller," he continued. "Ellison would want you to keep going, to honor his memory, at least. Because that's what we do. We're not here to save the world or even our country. We're here to save each other, the men like Ellison we fight beside."

"I get that, I really do. But..." Miller hung his head. "Every time we go outside the wire, I'm so damn fucking scared."

"Let you in on a secret. We all are fucking terrified. Anyone tells you different is lying. But we all know there's too many lives depending on us keeping our shit together, keeping our head in the game, as crap as this game is." His expression softened slightly. "I know it's not fair, but this is the shit show we've all been dealt. All we can do is make the best of it. Fight as hard as we can so we all get to go home. Alive."

Miller, god bless him, seemed to buy into Blake's Dr. Phil meets Oprah emotional psychobabble. Not that Blake didn't mean every word of what he'd said, but words were meaningless out here, no defense against bullets and shrapnel.

Blake stood. "Enough talk, let's show them. Make 'em pay for all the Ellisons and Bukoskis. Ready to get to work, soldier?"

Miller nodded, his gaze still distant, but he stood up, and they walked out together.

~

THE RG-31 VEHICLES ROLLED OUT, billowing dust in their wake. The rising sun painted the barren landscape in hues of gold and red as they made their way toward the highway and the village. The radio crackled with chatter from other units, but so far, all was quiet.

Blake tensed as their convoy turned onto Highway 1. The infamous "Highway to Hell" stretched from Kabul to Kandahar, cutting a swath of asphalt across the harsh Afghan landscape. It was also a dangerous stretch of Taliban activity.

The tension ratcheted up a notch among his squad. The banter soon ceased, and the vehicle became silent, apart from the hum of the engine.

Miller fidgeted with his rifle, his eyes darting from one side of the road to the other before catching Blake's. He nodded, attempting to reassure the kid.

The convoy rumbled along, each bump and pothole sending a jolt through the vehicle. Blake scanned the roadside ahead, looking for signs of digging, suspicious debris, or any other unexplained anomaly in the dirt that might hint at buried explosives.

Corporal Rodriguez's voice crackled over the radio in his helmet. "All clear on the right flank, Sarge."

"Copy that," Blake responded, his gaze never leaving the road.

They passed the burned-out hulk of a car with twisted metal and a scorched shell, a stark reminder of the dangers on this stretch of highway. Sweat beaded on Blake's forehead, as they approached a narrow pass between two hills.

He keyed his mic. "All units, tighten formation. Possible choke point ahead."

The convoy slowed, vehicles drawing closer together. Tension radiated from his squad. Miller's knuckles were white on his weapon, while Specialist Lee's eyes darted constantly between her sector and the rocky outcroppings on the hills above. Then the landscape flattened, and a scattering of buildings on either side of the highway lay ahead.

A plume of dust in the distance caught Blake's attention. He squinted, trying to make out the source. "Vehicle approaching. Stay sharp."

The dust cloud grew larger, becoming a battered pickup truck speeding toward them.

Blake's eyes narrowed as the truck stopped, partially blocking the convoy's path ahead. The lone driver remained seated, his intentions unclear as they approached. If they stopped to inspect the driver and his truck, the entire convoy would be sitting ducks for any snipers. Blake's mind raced through potential scenarios. Was this a civilian in distress? A Taliban scout? Or something worse? The few months he had spent in this unforgiving terrain had taught him to trust his instincts, and right now, every fiber of his being screamed danger.

He re-scanned the surrounding area through the

window's slit, looking for any signs of an ambush or hidden threats, before moving to the rear doors.

"Halt while I see what this guy's—"

A deafening roar shattered the air, followed by a blinding flash. The world lurched violently, spinning with the sickening crunch of metal and glass. Blake was thrown into the air, his body a rag doll in the chaos. His head struck something hard as he hit the asphalt. Darkness threatened to overtake him, but somehow, he clung to consciousness. An acrid smell of burning rubber and fuel filled his nostrils as he struggled to regain his bearings, his mind reeling from the sudden assault on his senses.

Through the haze of dust and smoke, Blake could make out that their once sturdy RG-31 truck was now reduced to a mangled ruin.

A muffled, pitiful moan cut through the incessant, loud ringing in Blake's ears. He lay sprawled on the baking hot asphalt, every breath a laborious effort.

Pain lanced through his leg where shrapnel had lodged deep into the flesh. He tried to move but found his body unresponsive, pinned by wreckage. Panic surged, adrenaline momentarily numbing Blake. He forced himself to focus—to assess.

He registered fragmented images—Rodriquez slumped lifelessly in his seat that had blown out of his vehicle, both his legs gone. Miller's face twisted in agony as he clutched at a gruesome wound just a few yards from him.

"Miller...No, Miller..." Blake's voice came out a rasping whisper, barely audible even to himself.

~

SEARING LIGHT.

A distant murmuring of indistinguishable voices.

Groans of pain.

Blake's eyes opened, squinting as he did so. A fluttering wall of fabric and the rhythmic beeping of monitors slowly came into focus. His lower body ached. He blinked, trying to piece together what had happened. He looked down to see his right leg bandaged, then noticed his arms and hands crisscrossed by shrapnel wounds.

A nurse approached his bedside. "Sergeant Harrow, you're at the Kandahar Airfield hospital, transferred from FOB Lagman. How are you feeling?"

Blake opened his mouth to speak, but his throat felt like sandpaper. The nurse offered him a sip of water through a straw. As he drank, memories of the ambush flooded back. His eyes widened with sudden urgency.

"My squad…Rodriguez…Johnson…Miller," he croaked.

The nurse's expression softened. "I'm sorry, Sergeant. You were the only survivor from your squad."

Blake felt as if he'd been punched in the gut. He shook his head in disbelief. A flash of memory came to him. "No…that can't be right. I saw Miller…he was alive…"

Just then, one of the medical team members came by, his face grave. "Sergeant Harrow, I'm Captain Kwan, one of the surgeons here," he said, glancing at the nurse, who excused herself before moving away. Kwan took a chair next to Blake's bed. "I was told that Private Miller was brought in alive to Lagman, but his injuries were too severe. I'm sorry to say, he died shortly after arrival." He cleared his throat. "That was three days ago. The combat surgical team at Lagman stabilized you and transferred you here. You've been drifting in and out of consciousness since arrival."

Blake closed his eyes, squeezing them tight, as the reality of what happened crashed over him. His squad and his friends were all gone. All dead. And he was still here. Still alive.

Kwan continued, "Do you remember anything about what happened?"

Blake kept his eyes closed. Shook his head, releasing a fresh wave of pain. He felt more than remembered flying through the air, the blast wave slapping him down, but mostly…Miller's face. "No."

"That's to be expected. We've had this conversation several times since you arrived, so don't be alarmed if you forget it again—it will take time. You've sustained several superficial shrapnel wounds and the tissue of your right thigh had some deeper damage, all easily treated. However, our main concern is that you've suffered concussive brain trauma."

Blake opened his eyes and gazed blankly at the curtain surrounding his bed. "Concussion? That's nothing. Send me back in, coach."

"I'm afraid it's not that simple. The CT scan hasn't shown any bleeding around your brain or swelling severe enough to require operation." He almost sounded regretful that he hadn't had the opportunity to slice open Blake's head. "But your symptoms and our scans show signs of deeper damage. Brain contusion—a bruise, you might say. I've arranged for you to be transferred to Landstuhl tomorrow. They have more advanced imagining capabilities and can design a course of rehabilitation before you're sent back home."

Blake barely registered the doctor's words. Except the last one. *Home.* A concept that now felt so foreign. How the hell was he supposed to go home when his brothers-in-arms would never see their families again? Reality seeped in, and he felt a numbness spread across his body. "You're sending me home…for a brain bruise?"

"Sergeant Harrow," Kwan began gently, "your injuries may not be visible, but trust me, they are serious. There could be lasting effects on cognitive function and memory."

Blake's head pounded with a dull ache, the doctor's words washing over him. Forgetting the look on Miller's face…that might be a blessing. But somehow it felt more like a betrayal. After all, Blake was the only one left alive to remember Miller and the others.

"Concussive brain injuries are the most difficult to treat," Kwan continued. "The damage is microscopic. Tearing of the tiny blood vessels, shearing of the brain tissue. Nothing I can operate on. No quick fix. But we do have therapies and with time and rest, you will see improvement."

Blake stared at him blankly, the surgeon's words echoing, slipping through his grasp, yet oddly familiar. They'd had this conversation before, hadn't they?

Kwan sighed and stood. "Get some rest, Sergeant. I'll check back later."

He left and the nurse returned. "Did Dr. Kwan explain everything?"

"Yeah," Blake muttered, his tone laced with bitterness. "Everyone's dead except me."

Chapter Seven

FRIDAY, *February 13th, 8:04 P.M.*

MERCER'S VISION danced with red spots as he squinted at Watts's form silhouetted by the spotlight on the landing above. Watts was now in his seventies, but he aimed the shotgun with a steady hand.

"Mercer." Watts didn't sound too surprised. Given his home-grown defenses, he'd clearly been expecting someone. Had he spotted Mercer during his earlier recon visit? "Thought you was locked up. Where you belong."

Mercer held up one hand to block the spotlight exposing their position. "We came for what's rightfully ours. Hand the rubies over, and we promise we won't hurt you, old man."

Watts snorted with derision. "You don't know the half of it. Well, come and get them, if you can!"

A gunshot sped past Mercer, but he wasn't the target. The slug splintered a two-by-four braced against a large, eight-foot-high bookshelf packed with cinderblocks and small appliances. The whole lot suddenly collapsed, burying Brick in an avalanche of junk.

Mercer fired up at Watts's position with a rapid series of cracks, shredding the wooden banisters before finally hitting the spotlight and plunging the house back into darkness.

"Connor, get him outta there," he ordered his brother to help Brick while Mercer got back on the radio. "Alpha to Beta. What's your goddamn status?"

A reply crackled back. "We've made a way through the kitchen. Found a back staircase."

"Hold your position in case he tries to escape that way." Mercer repositioned his night vision googles. "Where's the thermal imager?"

Connor had lifted the shelf aside and helped Brick back up to his feet. Brick brushed a palm over his now dust-covered mohawk, then fished out the imager from beside an ancient waffle iron. Mercer took one look and saw the screen was cracked as well as the housing. Damn thing was dead.

"Fucking great." He tossed it back on the floor and touched his radio mic.

"It's Alpha. I think he's headed to the top floor, get your ass up there. We'll follow from this side. Over."

"Copy, out."

Mercer scanned the area through his goggles, looking for the easiest way through the mountains of junk. "Here, this way."

He shoved a chair aside and edged along the perimeter, skirting more debris, heading toward a closed door—a closet beneath the steps—and the landing beyond it. The others followed, forming up to keep an eye on the balcony above them.

Mercer reached the landing at the bottom of the staircase, clambered onto the dresser blocking his way, and jumped over. He checked the level above, then methodically moved up the steps, aiming his weapon to meet any potential threats with gritted teeth. Connor and Brick trudged behind him.

At the top of the first flight of stairs, Mercer jabbed a finger toward the doors on the right, silently ordering his brother and Brick to check them. Down a short hallway across from him, he spotted a metal circular staircase leading to the top floor—that was where the servant's staircase must come up from the kitchen, he thought. Which meant the rest of his team should have it covered from below.

Down the main hallway, the front staircase continued up, forming an atrium that was topped high above by a fancy wrought-iron skylight. Closer to him was a heavy oak door, slightly ajar, darkness behind it. He moved alongside the doorframe with a predator's grace. His gloved hand gently brushed the wood, feeling for any vibrations or sounds from within.

Nothing.

He glanced back at Connor and Brick, who stacked up behind him, their weapons at the ready. Connor nodded, his face tight with anticipation, while Brick adjusted his grip on his weapon.

Mercer leaned in closer to the door, straining to hear any sign from Watts—a slight creak of floorboards, rustle of clothing, anything. But the room beyond was eerily silent.

He gave a final, deliberate nod, then pushed the door open, stepping to the side to allow Brick to rush in first, weapon at the ready. Brick moved with surprising agility for his large frame, sweeping the shotgun left and right, covering every angle. Connor followed close behind, gaze sweeping through the shadows. Mercer was the last to enter, intensely scanning the room that was scattered with old, worn furniture and piled-up storage crates. Too many hiding places for Mercer's liking.

A creaking of boards from the hallway broke his focus, and he ran back out just in time to see Watts heading toward the circular back staircase. As Mercer raised his weapon, a shotgun blast came from the stairs, ripping a hole in the wooden paneling behind him.

Mercer ducked, ready to return fire, then stopped himself.

He needed Watts alive to find the jewels.

"He's going up the rear steps," he said into the radio to the team downstairs. "Get up here!"

Connor and Brick rejoined him, and they cautiously cleared the hallway leading to the spiral staircase Watts had run up. The rest of the team came up the stairs below, guns at the ready. He waved to them. Last thing he needed was to get shot by his own guys.

Now with reinforcements, he climbed the narrow spiral stairs. Watts had made a lethal mistake—he was trapped, nowhere to go unless he had a helicopter waiting on the roof.

Mercer had spent years pacing a cell, dreaming of this exact scenario. Watts would get what was coming to him, and Mercer would finally get the rubies that were rightfully his.

Halfway up, a loud thud came from above.

And another.

Mercer's eyes widened at the sight of a large wardrobe tumbling toward him. He stumbled backward back down the steps before slamming straight into Connor, who was close behind. They had no choice but to jump over the iron railing to the hallway below. The wardrobe slammed into a vertical support beam with a loud bang, the bottom corner jutting out toward them, completely wedged in, blocking their way.

Mercer swore as he rose to his feet. The others, Brick and the second team, were now all standing in the hallway, looking to Mercer for instruction.

Mercer opened fire with his MP5 in short bursts, emptying a magazine and reloading, using another until it too ran dry, ripping the wardrobe into shards. Then he waved his men forward, and they cleared the remnants of wardrobe, tossing the wood onto the hallway floor until a gap appeared. He resumed the chase, sprinting up the steps, followed by his men. They fanned out along the corridors surrounding the top floor atrium, finding more doorways and possible hiding places.

Mercer held up his hand as he heard a faint creaking noise from one of the rooms. He headed through the first door, barrel first, scanning the room through the green hue of his NVGs while swinging the barrel of his weapon from left to right.

A door at the end of the room, closing.

Fuck!

Mercer sprinted across the space, reaching it in seconds. The thick metal door was almost shut. He wedged his rifle butt into the space just in time to stop its latching. Through the gap, Watts desperately tried to hammer the MP5 loose with the butt of his shotgun.

Brick and Connor raced to help. Their combined brute strength pushed the door open. Mercer shoved his way inside, flinging Watts backwards. Before the old man could regain his footing, Mercer rushed in with a hard punch to the gut, sending Watts reeling onto the ground before scuttling away.

"Where are they?" Mercer demanded. "Give us the

rubies, and we'll let you live. Hold out, and I'm cutting off your fingers one by one."

Connor appeared alongside Mercer. "We haven't much time," he whispered.

Mercer nodded, not taking his gaze from Watts, who moved to sit up against one of the safe room's walls. The tiny space, probably once a closet, was filled to the max with the four men.

"You know they're cursed," Watts said. "Those jewels are bad news. They've got some curse on whoever holds 'em. Your grandfather told us. Right before your dad killed him."

"What the fuck are you talking about?" Mercer growled.

Watts let out a humorless laugh. "Oh, you didn't know? Stealing them was your old man's idea. I was only along for the ride. Jamie got into a big fight with your grandpa and killed him. But then your dad turned on me, tried to kill me, so I took the Stars and ran. Damn things ruined my life."

There was a stunned silence.

Watts held up one clenched hand and opened his fingers to reveal five brilliant rubies. "Ruined my life, after they ruined your dad's. He killed your granddad. The rubies drove him insane with greed."

Mercer gritted his teeth, fury boiling through him. "That's complete bullshit. How dare you, how fucking dare you!"

Watts fixed him a level stare. "Like it or not, Andy, it's the truth. As for the rubies, they've never done me any good. You boys are welcome to 'em."

With a flick of his wrist, Watts tossed them at Mercer, who couldn't help but follow them with his gaze, straining to see where they landed in the ghostly vision the NVGs provided.

Watts pulled a pistol with his other hand.

A loud bang filled the small space.

Mercer didn't even think, he spun back, raised his weapon and pumped a series of rounds into Watts's chest and head.

When he was finally done, Mercer shouted at the slumped, lifeless, and bloody pulp on the floor. "Eat that, you fuck!" He slowly lowered his weapon and turned. "Now let's find those—"

Mercer stopped and stared, dumbfounded, at his brother, on the ground, clutching his belly with blood-drenched fingers.

Chapter Eight

FRIDAY, February 13th, 8:17 P.M.

"CONNOR!"

Mercer dropped to his knees, staring down at his brother, whose face was getting paler by the second. "Fuck, no, no, no!" he stuttered.

That bastard Watts had caught Connor with a bullet just below the vest.

This was bad.

Mercer looked up at Brick, who stood by the safe room door, looking stunned. "Jeez, that was a lucky shot," Brick muttered.

"We gotta get him to a hospital," Mercer said urgently. He called to his other men standing outside the door to the closet-sized room. "Make a stretcher, help me get him to the van."

Brick came to his senses and rushed out, taking charge of the men.

Mercer dug a bandana from his coat pocket, used it to

apply pressure. Connor groaned. "It's gonna be okay bro, it's…" Mercer started, then realized Connor was pushing something into his hand and looked to see his little brother's bloody hand pressing the jewels into his palm.

"I got 'em, bro," Connor croaked.

Mercer was tempted, so tempted. But the rubies represented Connor's future as much as his own. Positioning his body so none of the men could see, he took the jewels, carefully buttoning them into Connor's chest pocket. "You keep them safe for us both," he whispered.

The blood kept coming, pooling on the floor, and Mercer had no choice but to press harder against the wound. Connor cried out, his face growing pale, appearing ghostly in the NVGs. Mercer wished he could spare a hand and the time to find a freakin' light switch, but he couldn't let up for a moment.

"We're gonna get you help, okay, bro, listen to me," Mercer whispered. "Hey, look at me! You gonna live, no dying on me! You understand?"

Connor, tears welling up in his eyes from the pain, squeezed his eyes closed. "No…no dying," he gasped. Connor grabbed his brother's sleeve with weak fingers. "Don't…let me…die."

"You ain't dying!" Mercer vowed.

Brick, Harper, and Leon lifted Connor onto a door they'd taken off its hinges. Connor groaned and cried out in pain again.

"Careful, careful," Mercer ordered. He turned to the other crew members, Mark and Tyson. "Clear a path through that crap down there. Go!"

Getting Connor through the maze of piled up junk and out of the mansion into the back of the van seemed to take forever, but they made it.

"Hey, boss, don't mean to cut to the chase, but you

got what you came for?" Brick asked as Mercer hopped into the driver's seat while the others cared for Connor in the rear. He tried to sound casual, but Mercer wasn't fooled.

"Yeah, I got them. Now tell me the fastest fucking way to a hospital."

"Eastfork," Brick replied from the passenger seat, squinting at his phone map app. "Eastfork Medical Center."

Mercer drove as fast down the unplowed drive as he could in the terrible conditions, but every bump caused Connor to howl in pain. As they pulled onto the two-lane road, headlights approached them.

"That's a goddamn security guard," Brick muttered. "Talk about bad luck."

The security vehicle flashed its lights and half turned in the narrow road, completely blocking their way.

"Goddamn it," Mercer's growled under his breath. He turned his head and shouted to the rest of the crew. "We've company. Hold tight!"

Mercer tensed his grip on the steering wheel and picked up speed. The van hit the rear quarter panel of the security car with a loud crack. Then Mercer revved the engine, forcing the smaller vehicle into a culvert along the side of the road.

Mercer sped up again and glanced over his shoulder to the back of the van. "How's Connor doing?"

Tyson looked up with a grimace, his hands firmly pressed on Connor's wound. "I dunno, man. He don't look good. We gotta get to this hospital quick."

Mercer sped as best he could on the treacherous, slushy surface, finally turning onto a plowed four-lane highway. At last, a chance to pick up speed. Still, the windshield wipers struggled to clear the relentless snowfall, making the headlights nearly useless and visibility limited to a few feet beyond the van's hood.

In the rearview, a blue flashing caught Mercer's attention. "Dammit."

"What is it?" Brick asked.

"Looks like we got some local pigs on our ass. Alright, everyone, weapons ready. Tyson, stay with my brother, you got that?"

"No problem, Alpha," came the reply.

The sound of the automatic rifles, handguns and MP5s getting checked and reloaded filled the van interior.

Through the blizzard, a sign warning of a narrow, two-lane bridge ahead came into view. Mercer gripped the wheel hard against the buffeting wind, his eyes darting to the rearview and the State Police vehicle in pursuit. The vehicle gained on them rapidly. They were in the wrong vehicle for this shit.

More distant lights in the rearview. More cops.

Mercer shouted at Brick. "Get 'em off our ass!"

As the nearest police cruiser moved to try and get past them before the lanes reduced to two, Brick rolled down the passenger side window, leaned out with his rifle, and sprayed the police car with bullets. The pursuit vehicle braked, hitting a patch of ice before completely losing control and slamming hood-first into a snowbank.

Mercer nodded with approval, but their small victory was short-lived. Suddenly, the headlights revealed a State Police cruiser ahead of them, blocking the entrance to the two-lane bridge.

Ramming them was the only option. "Hold on!" he shouted as he accelerated hard.

The statie's lights started flashing, and two troopers jumped out, drawing their sidearms. One cop fired, but the van was closing in on them too quickly.

The front of the van smashed into the first cop with a heavy thump and sent him flying into the air. Mercer swerved and smashed into the cruiser, spinning both vehicles into a skid. The cruiser crashed into the bridge abutment, while Mercer desperately tried to control his fishtailing vehicle and avoid the obstacles on the side of the road.

A sudden jolt sent shockwaves through his bones, his stomach lurching as the van hit something and stopped moving.

"Fuck!" someone shouted.

Connor screamed in agony.

As Mercer came to his senses, he realized the engine had died, but the headlights remained on, illuminating a cluster of trees along the roadside. They'd spun a one-eighty, now facing back the way they had come, at an angle. Blurred red and blue flashing from more approaching law enforcement vehicles grew brighter through the swirling blizzard. Mercer killed the van lights. As his eyes adjusted to the darkness, he noticed movement in his door mirror—the second trooper struggling to regain his footing in the deep snow.

Mercer reached for his Glock and slipped out of the vehicle, an icy wind hitting his face like a harsh slap. The trooper had disappeared behind the crashed cruiser where he was probably calling for backup or grabbing more weapons. Either way, he had to die—or else Mercer and the van would be caught in a crossfire when the other cops arrived.

"Dammit." Mercer banged on the side of the van. "Everyone out except you, Tyson, stay with Connor," he commanded. "Take positions and keep in radio contact. We got cops, at least two cars coming down the road. Harper, try and get this piece of shit started."

The rear doors flung open. Four of the men filed out and fanned across the road into concealed positions where the road narrowed from four lanes to two.

"Protect the van," Mercer ordered. "I'll get the trooper."

Tyson stayed with Connor in the back while Harper tried to get the engine going, but as Mercer stalked after the cop, all he heard was the sound of an engine turning but refusing to spark to life.

As he approached the rear of the cruiser in a stoop, Mercer held his weapon in both hands. Even with night vision, he couldn't see jack-shit in the storm. He moved across the narrow bridge to the end of the barrier wall and stopped, focusing on the location of his last sighting of the cop. Seeing no movement, except the blur of snowfall, he continued past the cruiser and into the tree line along the river bank. He took slow steps, swinging his weapon's barrel left and right, until he heard a distinct crack and caught sight of a figure moving fast through the brush. Mercer fired twice at the blur, and the figure dropped.

"Gotcha," he cried, triumphantly. He hurried to the spot, his boots crunching in the thick snow, and looked down at the uniformed State Police officer staring lifelessly up into the sky, two wounds in his chest, including one directly over his heart.

From the bridge, the muffled crack of gunfire from MP5 bursts cut through the howling wind. Mercer hurried back to the van. Two county sheriff cars had come to a halt about twenty yards away. His men were engaging from either side of the road, the deputies taking cover behind their vehicles and returning fire.

Mercer poked his head into the rear of the van.

Harper turned around from the driver's seat. "Ain't starting, Alpha. Just won't go."

"Shit! Help the others."

"How the fuck are we getting out of here?" Tyson asked.

"We'll get out of here," Mercer replied sternly. Then louder for the sake of Connor, he said, "Hang in there! Ya hear me?"

A faint moan slipped from Connor's lips.

Mercer looked at Tyson. A hard look that telegraphed exactly what would happen to the man if he didn't obey. "Stay with him. I'll be right back."

He grabbed two new magazines for his rifle and exited the way he had come in, through the back doors. He sprinted in a crouch over to the left tree line and crept through the woods, out of sight from the police vehicles. His heart pounded as his adrenaline picked up, the cracking of gunfire adding to his buzz. He wondered if he should have brought Harper or one of the others with him as support.

Too late. No, he was good. This felt good.

The howling wind and blizzard conditions easily covered his approach. When he reached a spot parallel to the police vehicles and cops firing back at his men, he found himself in a perfect location. Snow-covered bushes provided cover with a clear view of the targets. He assessed the targets through his NGV's. Four cops, two behind each vehicle.

No, five.

One still inside a county sheriff's SUV parked farther back, radioing for back-up.

Shit. Need to move fast on this one.

"Alpha to Squad," he whispered into his radio, "go, go, go!"

As Mercer moved toward the rear vehicle, on his flank he saw Leon burst from cover, sprinting forward in a low crouch, while Brick and Mark laid down suppressing fire.

Leon shouted, "Set!"

From the other side of the road—now in the cops' blind spot—Brick exploded into motion. "Flash out!"

As the flash popped in an explosion of light, Mercer removed his NVGs, then took aim with his rifle at the cop who was farthest back from the rest. He fired once but missed.

Shit!

He'd underestimated the wind, which was stronger than he'd thought. The cop realized and turned in his direction, bringing her pistol to bear on him.

Mercer was quicker. He fired and hit the target this time, dropping the officer.

Shouts of alarm broke through the wind as Mercer's men engaged the remaining cops. Now that he'd out-flanked them, it was easy pickings. He sighted his next target and hit the officer in the neck and head. The man fell to the ground.

His partner, on the other side of their vehicle, fired at one of Mercer's approaching men, hitting her target. The black-clad figure fell onto the snow with a grunt of pain.

Mercer moved in and fired point-blank, killing the officer immediately with a callous pop to the head. Another body hit the ground.

The remaining two cops huddled behind the last cruiser. An MP5 opened up, smashing the car's windshield and ripping the tires to shreds. Mercer crouched low and used the chaos to maneuver around behind the cops and fired.

And then it was over. The gunfire stopped, leaving only the blizzard's howling wind.

"Get Connor into the SUV," Mercer shouted over the radio.

Soon, they were all crowded inside the vehicle, Connor draped over the back seat, no longer speaking but able to squeeze Mercer's hand when he checked on him.

"What about Mark?" Brick asked as they drove past a man on the ground clutching his leg next to a dead cop.

"Got no more room," Mercer replied coldly, revving the engine. "Find me another route to the hospital." The SUV accelerated down the road.

Brick pulled up the map and showed him. Mercer found the buttons that turned the police lights and siren on —now no one could stop him from saving Connor.

Chapter Nine

FRIDAY, February 13th, 8:36 P.M.

AFTER SUFFERING another finger prick and Alyssa calling med control with Thomas's labs and getting a treatment plan, they loaded Thomas onto the carry chair and began down the steps. Blake was glad Alyssa had decided to wait until they were in the ambulance before starting an IV. Thomas was a difficult stick, and he'd hate to have an IV jostled out by the steep steps.

"And how's you, son?" Thomas asked Blake as they rounded the first landing. "Still out there trying to save the world, like always?"

Blake chuckled lightly. "Sometimes it feels like I'm putting one fire out just for four more to ignite."

"Can't fix everything on your own. You're not a superhero."

Blake raised his eyebrow and dipped his mouth with mock disappointment. "Whaddaya mean, I'm no superhero? C'mon, Blake-man would make a great comic book character."

"You mean comedy character," Alyssa corrected.

Thomas laughed, which morphed into a hacking cough. When he had finished, he rasped in a deep breath. "Er, jeez, sorry. Swallowed wrong."

"Take it easy there." Alyssa reached for his pulse as they took another pause at the next landing.

"My bad," Blake said. They resumed climbing down the steps. "I should know better. Especially giving away my secret identity."

Thomas looked toward Alyssa while pointing at Blake. "When are you getting this one put away? Hope it's soon."

"I'm on it," she replied, smirking.

"Seriously, though," Blake said, changing the topic away from his personal life. "It's tough seeing people struggle and knowing I can't do more for them."

"True, true." Thomas shifted slightly in the chair. It wasn't the most comfortable mode of transportation no matter how careful Blake and Alyssa were. "But instead of chasing every problem, focus on the small victories. Like the time you saved that kid with the asthma attack. That was a big deal."

"Yeah, it was. Just…" He exhaled slowly. "I still feel like I could've done more, you know?" Jeez, what was it about Thomas that had him sharing shit he didn't even admit to himself?

Thomas's tone was serious but gentle. "Take it from someone who's been around the block a few times. You can drive yourself mad worrying about what you can't control."

It was true. And mirrored what every therapist and group Blake had ever been to said. He couldn't help it. He needed everything in its right place, the right box. All memories boxed up, a routine to take care of today, worries about tomorrow safely locked away.

"Yeah, I've been working on that."

When they reached the ground floor, Blake wheeled Thomas to the doors as Alyssa held them open, a gear bag slung over each of her shoulders. The snow had gotten heavier even though it actually felt a little warmer, maybe because the wind had shifted direction.

Once Thomas was strapped onto the ambulance's gurney and their gear was stowed, Blake hopped into the driver's seat and turned them around to head to the hospital in Potsdam.

In the back, Alyssa began an IV. First stick, Blake noted with approval. Not easy to do on Thomas.

"There you go, all set," she said, adjusting the IV fluids.

"So, who won the bet?" Thomas asked, cracking a grin.

Alyssa laughed. "Well, neither, actually. Dr. Sara went for high sugar and Blake here was counting on your kidneys to win him those M&M's."

In the rearview, Blake saw Thomas gesture for Alyssa to lean closer to him. "Say, Blake and Dr. Sara. Any progress?"

"I heard that," Blake interjected.

"Don't be an idiot," Thomas told him. "Life is short. Ask the girl out. Otherwise, you'll end up just like me. All alone."

"Hey, you've got us," Alyssa protested. "And you got lucky, married the love of your life. Am I right?"

Thomas nodded with a rueful smile as his eyes drifted off to previous memories. "That I did, that I did. Bless her soul."

Blake brought the ambulance to a stop at the red light at the intersection with Route 37, ready to turn onto the main highway to Potsdam. It would have been tempting to run the red, sirens blasting, but Blake resisted. While he waited for the light to turn, he peered into the back.

Thomas was talking to Alyssa in a low voice, his face animated. She laughed, and Blake had the feeling Thomas was sharing one of his R-rated anecdotes from when he'd been in the Navy.

"Looks like you're feeling better," he told the older man.

Alyssa straightened up, assuming a professional expression. "Yep, we're all good. Vitals stable, blood sugar normal."

"Roads look like they're getting nasty," Thomas said. "You guys can just take me home, I'll be fine."

"You're not getting off that easy," Alyssa chided him. "Dialysis, remember? Not to mention you'll need an IV tonight, keep your sugar stable."

"Ugh." Thomas's face twisted in an exaggerated pout, worse than any toddler, making Blake smile. "They never let me get any sleep. All the noise and the nurses checking me every half an hour. And worse thing is, nowadays seems like half of them are men!"

"Ah, but still pretty, right?" Alyssa joked.

The light changed to green, but as Blake put his foot on the gas to cross, his peripheral vision caught the flashing lights of a speeding law enforcement SUV heading straight for the driver's side of the ambulance. He hit the brakes, sending the ambulance into a skid just as the SUV swerved to make an abrupt left turn.

"What the hell!" Alyssa shouted from the back.

As fast as it had appeared, the vehicle disappeared into

the blizzard. But why was a county sheriff's unit speeding toward Eastfork?

"You okay back there?" When Blake looked in the direction the SUV had come from, he spotted more familiar red and blue lights glinting through the snowfall. None of them moving.

"Yeah, all good." Alyssa replied. She checked on Thomas once more, but he waved her away. She climbed up front to join Blake. "What's going on?"

Blake tried the radio, but it gave him nothing but crackles and pops. "Call dispatch," he told Alyssa who was already sliding her cell free. "If that was an injured cop, they were heading in the wrong direction."

"Any officers around here know not to go to Eastfork," she said as the call connected. "Wayne? You hear anything about police casualties or any major trauma event?"

She put it on speaker and held it between them. Wayne, the EMS dispatcher, answered, "There was chatter earlier about state troopers in pursuit of possible robbery suspects, and the county guys were coming to back them up, but then everything went quiet."

"Maybe they changed channels," Blake said. Something usually reserved for critical incidents requiring private communications.

Alyssa met Blake's gaze with a frown, then told Wayne, "Seems like one of the deputies is heading to Eastfork, maybe with a casualty. You might want to warn Sara."

Blake leaned toward the phone. "I can see several more units on 37, near the bridge—but they're not moving, looks from here like they're across the whole road, blocking it."

"You're our only unit available," Wayne said. He didn't spell it out, but it was clear he was leaving it up to them to decide: follow protocol and leave with Thomas, prioritizing their patient's need to get to Potsdam…or possibly enter an unsecured scene to rescue potential injured law enforce-ment officers.

Blake and Alyssa had an entire argument with a few looks, shakes of the head, raised eyebrows, jerks of the chin back toward Thomas, and assorted scowls.

"Thomas is our responsibility," Alyssa finally said, pulling rank.

From the rear, Thomas raised his voice. "If you leave hurt policemen lying in the snow just to get me to a hospital bed I don't even want, I swear to god not only won't I ever speak to either of you again, when I die, I'm gonna come back and haunt you for the rest of your lives!"

Good enough for Blake. He checked the intersection and turned in the direction of the police vehicles.

Alyssa sighed and spoke into the phone, "Wayne, let the cops know we're approaching the scene to assess. Have their dispatcher call the units involved, tell them our radio is out so they'll need to go through you for comms. I'll keep the line open." Then to Blake, "Slow, maintain a safe distance."

Clearly Alyssa had never been in a gun battle. They were already past a "safe" distance. But Blake's gut told him this scenario was all wrong. Best he hoped for was that they'd find cops living but hurt, because the other option…

"Remember the first rule of EMS," Alyssa reminded him.

"Don't become a victim yourself," he answered grimly.

As they approached, they identified a dark shape in the snowy ground, far from any vehicle. Blake hit the high beams and the exterior spotlight, aiming it past the motionless form to the ground near the two cruisers ahead of them. Four more bodies that they could see. There could be more on the other side of the vehicles. He stopped the ambulance.

"Shit." Alyssa's grip on the phone tightened. "Wayne, we've got multiple officers down."

Blake admired the way her voice remained steady. For once, he wasn't as able to compartmentalize, a flash of memory overwhelming him. The snow-dusted asphalt became the sandy dust of that highway from hell in Afghanistan. The bodies of the officers were his comrades: Rodriquez, O'Leary, Miller writhing in pain…

Not Miller. An officer on the ground, clad in black SWAT gear, waving his arms.

Blake rolled his window down and stuck his head out. "Sir! Can you show your hands and identify yourself?"

"Officer Lopez. I've been shot in the leg."

"Is the gunman still on scene?"

"No, they're all dead. Damnit, I'm bleeding out!"

Blake held his hand up to Alyssa, who was still on the phone, indicting for her to stay put. Before she could protest, he grabbed the trauma bag, opened the driver's door, and jumped out.

His boots crunched through the slushy snow as he approached the first body and quickly checked it for any signs of life: her eyes were open, a blood trail ran down her chin and neck while her skin was turning blue.

Blake had seen enough dead bodies to know he was staring at one. He approached a second officer, sprawled face down, handgun still gripped by icy fingers. Blake carefully moved the gun away, rolled the man over, felt for a pulse. Nothing.

"Hey, bud, hurry!" the wounded officer pleaded. But if he was able to scream like that, he wasn't as critically injured as an officer unable to call for help might be.

Blake began to move toward the man, but something he'd seen set alarm bells going in his brain. He glanced back, and his eyes fell on the dead officer's name badge: Lopez.

He turned to see the wounded "cop" rolling over to reveal an automatic rifle aimed right at him.

Blake slowly raised his hands.

"Don't move a muscle!" the man demanded as he struggled to his feet, leaving behind a large patch of blood in the snow where he had been lying.

Chapter Ten

FRIDAY, February 13th, 8:41 P.M.

SARA PLACED a plastic basin of hot water mixed with betadine on the floor near her tween-aged patient's grimy foot. Five years of residency training at one of the East Coast's busiest trauma centers put to good use, she thought.

"Evan, we'll need to let it soak for a while, soften the tissue around the ingrown toenail. Then I can take pack it with iodine gauze, and you'll be set."

The boy grunted, barely able to rip his eyes away from the game on his cellphone, and submerged his bare foot in the water. He winced and knifed a look at Sara, holding her responsible for his discomfort.

Sara returned a thin smile. Yet another satisfied customer. The bean counters at corporate HQ would be so happy.

Evan's mom, wrapped in a puffer coat and sporting a pulled-down woolen hat bearing a team insignia, sat on a chair in the examination room, talking to someone on her cell.

Sara exhaled silently. Only a matter of time before this place, her clinic, followed the rest of the hospital into oblivion. She thought about the local people and all the patients who relied on this facility—the elderly, the working poor, those without transport.

How were they going to get to Potsdam when they needed urgent care? The system had failed them, leaving the most vulnerable to fend for themselves. She had to keep the clinic running as long as possible for the sake of the community that depended on it. She wouldn't abandon her patients, not without a fight.

"Ingrown toenail. No, he won't be able to play, I don't think. He can barely walk, it hurts so bad. Hang on..." The mom looked at Sara. "Doctor, how's it looking? Will he be able to play hockey tomorrow?"

"Not tomorrow, but give it a few days and he'll be fine," Sara answered.

The mom shrugged and returned to her conversation just as Angie, the ward clerk, came rushing down the hallway. Sara stepped out of the treatment room to meet her.

"There's a police car coming up the road, lights and sirens," Angie said.

Sara frowned. "Here? They should definitely not be coming here. They know that."

"I know," Angie said. "Sorry." She fled back to the waiting area.

Sara walked briskly down the hall and entered the EMS dispatch center inside the ambulance bay. The tiny, glass-walled office overlooked the ambulance entrance with a second door out to the large garage that held the EMS vehicles and a resupply area.

Wayne, the dispatcher, a man in his fifties, swung

around on his gamer chair. His U-shaped desk had a stack of takeout coffee mugs with crumpled-up candy wrappers scattered around several computer monitors, a radio with a headset, and a multi-line phone.

"Wayne, did the cops radio in? What's the emergency? Why are they coming here?"

He shrugged. "Just got off with Alyssa. Said there was some kind of incident and they saw a cop car headed our way, running lights and siren. Getting ready to call county dispatch—"

Just as Wayne picked up his radio mic, the reflection of flashing red and blue lights in the office window grew stronger. Sara leaned forward to hit the button to raise the garage door, the sheriff's SUV barely clearing it as it roared into the ambulance bay and screeched to a halt. Its doors flew open, and five figures clad in SWAT gear climbed out.

One shouted, "Hey! We need a doctor! Someone's been shot."

"Wayne, grab the gurney from the trauma bay and send everyone this way," Sara ordered. The older man stared at her, mouth agape. "Do it, now!"

Once he rushed through the door leading into the ER —*minor* care clinic, she couldn't help the mental correction, especially as it meant she was seriously understaffed and under-equipped to handle any kind of gunshot wound— Sara strode into the bay to meet her patient. "I'm Dr. Porter. What happened?"

The men parted, gesturing for her to look into the rear seat. She noted that they all held rifles at the ready, as if anticipating an attack. She'd done a stint as trauma doc for the SWAT team in Toledo where she'd trained. These men felt hardened, like them. Still, something felt off…

She ignored the itch to focus on the armed men behind

her and approached her patient. Mid-twenties, pale, diaphoretic, obvious penetrating abdominal trauma with significant blood loss. Responded minimally to commands, maintaining airway, peripheral pulses thready and rapid. Ignoring the blood on her hands from assessing him, she crawled out of the passenger compartment.

The driver stood in her way, cradling his rifle, his posture taut, challenging her. "He's going to be okay, right? You have to save him."

She met his gaze, not liking his tone of command. "This isn't an ER any more. We're barely a minor care clinic. And he needs a Level One trauma center. The closest is Syracuse. With the storm, there's no way the helicopter will be flying. We'll stabilize him as best we—"

He shook his head, leaned into her space. "Not 'we,' Doc. *You.* You will stabilize him, fix him up, do whatever he needs done. Here. Now."

Sara wanted to shove him out of her way—she needed to get to work if her patient had any chance. Before she could move, Wayne came rushing in with the gurney, followed by Nick, her physician assistant, and Kelly, her nurse. The only other staff on the night shift were the desk clerk, an x-ray tech, and a security guard patrolling somewhere.

The cop turned, raised his rifle, pointing it at Wayne, who stopped short, raised his hands, the gurney rolling across the concrete floor. Two of the other cops caught it before it hit the SUV.

Sara wondered why they didn't move to load their injured comrade onto it—and realized that was what had been bothering her: SWAT team members and most patrol officers were trained in basic trauma care, even had trauma kits with the tools to stop excessive blood loss.

Yet all these guys had done was to use someone's

bandana as a pressure dressing. These guys weren't cops. Her mouth went dry as the adrenaline rush of a dealing with a GSW was overridden by the sheer, sudden terror that she was all that stood between life and death for everyone in the building.

The leader seemed to sense her distress. "Just so we're clear," he said, his rifle still aimed at Wayne. "You're gonna have multiple traumas on your hands if you don't save my brother."

She lowered her gaze as if submitting to his authority. "No need for that, officer," she said calmly. "We might not have much more than the basics here, but we—*I* will do everything in my power to save his life."

The leader looked at her for a second as if in contemplation, then slung the rifle over his shoulder and nodded. "Good." He stood aside as if inviting her to join a party. "Guess we shouldn't waste any time, then."

Sara and Nick wheeled the gurney to the SUV, and two of the armed men helped load the wounded patient onto it while the others watched, hands on their weapons.

"What's his name?" Sara asked.

"Con…Officer Connor," came the leader's reply.

"Wayne, we need to alert any patients who are waiting that we're treating a Code Black," Sara said, making deliberate eye contact with the dispatcher, who nodded and hurried ahead of them through the double doors into the hospital. If Angie could get the remaining patients through the waiting room exit and out of harm's way, that would be a load off Sara's mind.

"What the hell's a 'Code Black'?" the man asked suspiciously.

She looked at the man she assumed was the ringleader, as he had been doing all the talking and threatening. Did he know? Why would he if he wasn't a real police officer?

She inhaled, kept her voice steady. "It means we're treating a wounded police officer, and less urgent patients will have to wait or come back another time."

"Right. We take priority." He turned to one of his crew. "Hey, er, Officer Tyson, go help Wayne out, will ya? Make sure everyone stays calm and out of the doc's way."

Sara hid a grimace of disappointment. Her plan was toast already. But, on the plus side, they fell for her explanation of Code Black. It actually referred to an active shooter or hostage-taker.

As they began to wheel her patient, Connor, through the double doors, the ringleader ordered another one of his men to stay with their van. She overheard his quiet reply.

"Sure, Mercer."

The remaining four men followed Sara, Nick, and Kelly as they wheeled the gurney into the former trauma bay. Most of its equipment had been stripped out. However, there were still items useful for minor emergencies, plus the crash cart, which contained emergency medication and equipment for advanced life support protocols.

But there was no banked blood, no ultrasound, and no ventilator, which was going to make treatment a challenge, to say the least. Sara and her tiny team scrambled into action.

"Monitor, and let's get these clothes off," Sara ordered as she moved to the head of the gurney, ignoring her armed audience. "Get me two large bore IVs going."

As Nick moved to cut off Connor's layers of clothing and Kelly grabbed the monitor and leads, Sara placed a non-rebreather mask over his face. She leaned over him— god, he looked so young—and brushed the hair away from his face. "Can you open your eyes? Tell me your name?"

His eyelids fluttered open, then shut tight against the bright exam light shining above him. "C-Connor," he whispered.

"Good job, Connor. Tell me what hurts."

The leader, Mercer, suddenly grabbed Nick and wrenched him away. "Leave it!" he ordered, grabbing the pistol Nick had taken from Connor's belt. Then Mercer turned to Sara. "He's been shot in the belly. What the hell are you playing at?"

"ABCs," she said in a quiet tone, meeting his gaze easily. "Bullets don't stop once they're inside the body, they can go anywhere. I need to assess everything, starting with his airway, breathing, circulation, mental status…Want me to recite the full advanced trauma resuscitation guidelines, or shall I return to saving my patient's life?"

Without waiting for an answer, she turned back to Connor.

Mercer grabbed her arm, leaning next to her ear, whispering, "*Your* patient, *my* brother. Don't forget that." He nudged her between the ribs with his gun.

"You want me to save your brother, you need to give us room to work."

He stepped away and waved his men back, the guy with the ugly mohawk bending down to remove the weapons and ammunition Connor had carried along with his ballistic vest.

Nick cut away Connor's shirt, allowing Kelly to apply the monitor leads. One eye on the display, Sara palpated his cervical spine, then ran her hands down both sides of his chest, assessing for possible rib fractures and crepitus—signs that the bullet damaged a lung.

"You're doing great, Connor," she continued in a soothing tone. "Anything hurt up here?"

Connor shook his head.

"How about here?" She pressed on his belly, starting with the upper left quadrant. Connor winced, and again when she moved lower, then gave out a loud groan when she pressed in the area near the bullet wound.

"Christ," Mercer shouted, "give him something for the pain."

She wished she could, but there was nothing she had here to give him—the clinic didn't keep any injectable narcotics on site. "Kelly, how we doing with those IVs?"

"First one running." Kelly crossed behind Nick, who was cutting away Connor's pants, leaving him totally exposed.

"Let's roll him, then we'll get the second one going and a Foley." Sara glanced at Mercer, who had turned away from his brother's naked body. He was going to like the idea of a Foley catheter—a tube inserted in the urethra— even less, but without an ultrasound or CT, her diagnostic options were limited.

In the background, the intercom crackled into action, announcing, "Attention all patients. The staff is busy with a Code Black at this time. Please move to the waiting room. Thank you."

Carefully, they rotated Connor to his side. As Sara searched for an exit wound, she felt relief. Wayne must've bamboozled Mercer's guy into believing her Code Black explanation. Between him and Angie, maybe they could still get the patients out.

"No exit wound," she announced. They rolled Connor back.

"That's good, right?" Mercer asked.

"No. It means the bullet spent all its energy inside his body. The bleeding you see here is only the tip of the iceberg." Sara turned to Nick. "I saw some surgical sets left behind. They're in the storage closet. Grab anything labeled 'trauma' or 'vascular' and bring them. Oh, and grab as many towels as you can. I might need to open his belly."

Nick's eyes went wide at that. "On it," he said, moving toward the door. One of Mercer's men, the one with the mohawk, joined him, gun drawn.

"Kelly, open those packs of Kerlix and the widest Ace you can find, let's get a pressure dressing on this." Sara began packing the wound with saline-soaked sterile gauze, applying firm pressure that made her patient moan in pain. His breathing became more rapid and shallow.

"Hey, Doc, what's this about a Code Black?"

Sara glanced back at the door to see Luca, the security guard.

Time stopped.

Sara opened her mouth to warn him, but no words came.

Luca frowned at Sara, then his eyes darted to the other men. He froze, taking in the sight of three armed guys in SWAT gear staring back at him.

One of the gang moved first, raising his weapon.

"No!" Sara shouted.

Luca went for his sidearm. It wasn't even a gun, only a taser.

A rapid volley of gunfire erupted, deafening in the confined space.

Kelly screamed.

Luca jerked, bounced against the door jam, his taser falling, unfired, hitting the floor a second before the bulky weight of his body followed.

Sara ran to him, checking for vitals. One of the shots

had blown out half his skull—the impact of automatic weapon fire at such close range was devastating. She hadn't seen anything this bad since leaving Toledo.

She sat back on her heels. "He's dead."

Chapter Eleven

FRIDAY, February 13th, 8:43 P.M.

ALYSSA IMMEDIATELY KNEW something was wrong when she saw Blake raise his hands. It took her a moment, the snow was so thick as it whipped through the night, for her to realize that the police officer he'd tried to help was now pointing a gun at him.

Why would a cop do that? Unless he was the reason for the dead cops lying everywhere. Alyssa moved into the driver's seat with a half thought of ramming the man with the ambulance, but the gunman was too close to Blake.

She turned to her phone, but Wayne had hung up on her. Sonofabitch. Quickly, she dialed the county dispatcher.

"Update on our situation," Alyssa told him after identifying herself. She couldn't believe how calm she sounded, but that was part of the job: respond first, react later. "There's now an armed man pointing a weapon at my colleague. I believe he might be responsible for your dead officers."

"State police are on the way as well as Potsdam PD. They should be with you in twenty minutes."

"Twenty minutes?"

"They're coming from the other end of the county and with the storm. Are you in immediate danger?"

"No, but my partner is."

"Ma'am, you need to leave. You and your patient should vacate the area. Now. If the gunman is smart, he'll keep your partner alive as a hostage."

Alyssa shook her head. No. She couldn't just leave Blake…but the dispatcher was right, she was also responsible for Thomas.

"Buckle up, Thomas," she told him as she fastened her own seat belt.

BLAKE BREATHED in through his nose, the ice-cold air burning his nostrils, held it for four seconds, then exhaled through his mouth and repeated the combat breathing process as he assessed the situation, considering his best options as time slowed down. A bead of sweat pooled at the base of Blake's neck despite the freezing temperatures, but his heart slowed along with his breathing, giving him total focus. Old habits.

The gunman took an unsteady step toward Blake, then another. With the third, he hit a patch of ice and slipped, off balance for a brief instant.

Blake's instincts kicked in. With one swift motion, he swept the impostor's leg out from under him, sending him sprawling to the ground onto his back.

As he fell, the man fired wildly. Blake hit the cold asphalt and rolled behind the cop car. He caught sight of the ambulance.

Why was Alyssa still here? What the hell was she think-ing? Hadn't she seen the gunman?

He waved a hand, signaling for Alyssa to get out of there. The engine revved in response. Blake crawled around the police car. From his new vantage point, he saw the assailant struggle to regain his footing. More than ice was affecting his balance—he was losing blood, and his one leg didn't seem able to hold his weight.

Blake rose into a crouch, about to move around behind the impostor to tackle him, when the ambulance wheels spun in the slush, skidding to a stop a few feet away, the cruiser between him and the gunman. Alyssa to the rescue —even if it was against all the rules and the stupidest thing she could have done. Blake figured he'd have time to yell at her later.

He wrenched open the passenger door and jumped in. The impostor cop had hauled himself up, using the cruiser for support. Blake slammed the door shut. "Go, go!"

Alyssa yanked the ambulance into reverse and hit the gas, sending the vehicle screeching backward just as their assailant swung his rifle in their direction.

"Contact!" Blake pushed Alyssa's head down.

A shower of bullets peppered the ambulance wind-shield before it shattered completely, spewing pebbles of glass into the cabin and across the hood. Alyssa ducked down below the wheel, but Blake knew they had to keep moving.

He shoved the gearshift back into drive and reached his leg across the center console to stomp onto the accelerator, sending the ambulance jolting forward. While keeping his head as low as possible, he took the wheel. Alyssa pressed herself against the door to give him room. He steered in the direction of the gunman, bullets pinging relentlessly into the ambulance's walls.

With a sudden thud, the ambulance hit the impostor's body, sending him flying over the hood of the cruiser. The ambulance careened off the police car and skidded into a U-turn. Blake steered them back onto the road and drove a half mile down the road before pulling over into the empty parking lot of a strip mall. He heaved a breath in, adrenaline ebbing.

Safe, they were all safe.

"Did you get him?" Thomas called from the back.

Blake released his hands, clamped around the steering wheel, ignored the way they shook once they were free. "He's down, not sure if he's dead though. Guess that's a problem for the cops." He scooted back over to the passenger seat, then turned to Alyssa squashed between the door and the driver's seat. "It's okay, we're—"

Alyssa, her face pale and eyes in shock, held her hand up. Blood dripped down her palm.

Blake grabbed her arms, pulling her upright so he could check her for injuries. He didn't have to look hard, quickly finding the entrance wound in the right side of her chest.

Their eyes met in the dim glow of the dashboard.

She was blinking fast in disbelief. "Blake? I think I've been shot."

Chapter Twelve

FRIDAY, February 13th, 8:48 P.M.

SARA CLIMBED TO HER FEET, fighting for control, taking care not to slip in Luca's blood. He was a quiet man but always had a smile and baked pies for her staff when they had to work holidays. And…

She whirled on Mercer and his men. "You killed him!"

"It was him or me, Doc, and I always vote for me," came Mercer's nonchalant reply. "Now get back to work on Connor. Otherwise, more of your people will be visiting the morgue."

At that moment, Nick and Mr. Mohawk rushed into view on the other side of the door, Mohawk with his gun raised, ready for a shootout.

The thug stopped at Luca's body where it blocked the entrance to the trauma bay, glanced from it to Mercer. "Guess I missed all the fun." Then he forced Nick, arms stacked high with trauma supplies, to step over Luca. "Got the shit she asked for."

Kelly ran to help Nick with the bundles of surgical equipment while Sara returned to Connor. Supposedly to monitor him, but really because she needed a moment where she could safely turn her back to Mercer and his men, regain her focus. She had a patient, and he had to be her priority—at least now that her other patients and staff had hopefully safely escaped.

Please, Wayne. Please have gotten them out of here.

Mercer's radio went off. She glanced back, saw him fumble at his ear as if he'd expected it to be fed to him more covertly. Sara gave a silent cheer. Finally, something had gone wrong for the bad guys. And she could listen in on his plans.

"Tyson here," came over the radio. "I got the patients, a clerk, an x-ray lady, and the dispatch guy corralled. But from the staff roster, there's a guard somewhere on the loose—"

"Don't worry about him," Mercer said into the radio. He regarded his men. "Brick, grab the dispatcher, see if we can avoid more unwanted guests. Maybe he can spin some story, send them elsewhere."

"On it." Mohawk stepped back over Luca's body and vanished down the hallway.

Mercer frowned at the mess Luca was making. "Harper, move that body out of the way, then help Tyson secure the patients. Make sure you get them all—families as well."

The man gave a British-style salute and bent down, hauling Luca's body to the same corner where Connor's bloody clothing and gear had been piled. He rummaged around in the clothes, retrieved some ammunition, then left as well.

"Hey, one thing, Doc. How come he said it was a joke, the Code Black thing?" Mercer asked.

Sara froze with her back to him, dared not turn to face him. "Probably because since the main hospital closed, the cops don't come here anymore," she said as casually as she could muster. "Remember, we're not an ER."

"Right," came his slow reply. Then, "But you are an ER doctor? Someone who knows that advanced trauma shit you were talking about?" Translation: someone who could save his brother.

"I am. And part of that advanced shit is we'll be inserting a catheter into your brother's bladder." She held up the Foley for him to imagine exactly why male patients especially did not enjoy the procedure. "Not sure you'll want to watch either."

Was it terrible that she was glad to see him turn pale as he realized what they were about to do?

He moved to the doorway, stopped to aim his rifle at each of them in turn, but Sara and her team ignored him. Best way to deal with bullies, she'd learned.

"I'll be right outside the door, so don't try anything funny."

Sara reassessed Connor. His vitals were slightly improved after a fluid bolus, but still not great. "How you doing?" she asked him.

With glassy eyes, his head turned to view the spot where Luca's corpse had been. "I'm sorry."

She met his eyes. "Wasn't you that shot him. We're going to give you the best care possible, I want you to know that."

He nodded, reached a hand to grasp hers. "I know. Thanks."

"There's going to be a lot to stuff happening, and some of it will be painful. We don't have any pain meds here, I'm sorry. I could give you some sedation, but since we also don't have an operating room or scans, I need you awake to tell me if things get worse."

He grimaced. "Andrew wouldn't trust you if I'm asleep."

Yeah, she'd kinda figured that as well. Which meant she also couldn't intubate him. There were paralytics and seizure meds on the crash cart that she could use to knock him out, put a breathing tube down his throat if he went into respiratory failure, but doing that would probably get her and her staff, maybe the other patients, all shot.

Apparently, Connor agreed. Given that he knew his brother and these men, she wasn't about to argue.

"It's okay, Connor. We'll just need to go old school tonight. You ever see *M*A*S*H*?"

That got a small smile from him. "Hawkeye Pierce. That's you."

"Nah, he's funnier. But we both kick ass and will do anything for our patients." She glanced to the foot of the bed where Kelly was set up to insert the Foley. "You saw the catheter I showed your brother?"

"Looked like a garden hose. You really gonna ram that up my—"

"Yep. But with a ton of lube. After some soap that will feel real cold."

"Cold all over already."

A little hypothermia wasn't a terrible thing given his injuries, but Sara bet most of his feeling cold was due to shock rather than body temp. "After the Foley, I'm going to be removing the pressure dressing and trying to see where the bleeding is coming from and if the bullet nicked your intestine. So, I'm leaving for just a minute to scrub up, okay?"

He nodded, then squeezed his eyes shut as Kelly began prepping for the Foley. Sara was lucky she had a real ER nurse with her tonight. Kelly was moonlighting from her job at Potsdam to save money for her upcoming wedding. And Nick worked as an EMT before he got his physician assistant degree, so a little blood and guts didn't bother him. Well, probably not as much as the men pointing guns at him.

She moved to the scrub sink, using a brush to remove the dried blood from when she'd assessed Connor in the SUV. Nick joined her, making a point of not looking at her and barely moving his lips as he whispered below the sound of the running water. "You know he's not gonna make it."

Sara gave a tiny nod.

"We can't try to jump them, his guys will shoot the hostages."

She shook her head and stomped on his foot. Of course they couldn't try anything like that, they'd end up getting everyone killed. What did he think, this was a movie?

"So, what're we gonna do?" He glanced at her, eyes wide.

"We're going to do our jobs. Focus on our patient." She hesitated, not wanting to tempt him into playing super-hero. "And pay attention to everyone. Sooner or later, they'll screw up."

"How can you be so sure?"

"Because they wouldn't be here if they hadn't already."

Chapter Thirteen

FRIDAY, February 13th, 8:49 P.M.

BLAKE PULLED Alyssa across the front seat and carried her into the rear compartment. Thomas was already yanking his monitor leads off, struggling to get free of them so he could move off the gurney.

"Hang on," Blake told Alyssa, setting her on the bench seat opposite the gurney.

He unbuckled Thomas, moved the IV to hang from a ceiling hook, then transferred Thomas to the bench as well, where Blake attached the oxygen tubing to a portable tank. He grabbed a few mylar emergency blankets and handed them to the old man to wrap himself in. With the front windshield blown out, the temperature was dropping fast inside the ambulance. They needed real shelter and medical facilities. But first he needed to stabilize both his patients.

"You okay, Thomas?"

"I'm fine, fine. Help Alyssa."

It was tight quarters, but Blake picked Alyssa up and arranged her on the gurney, quickly got her on oxygen, removed her jacket, unbuttoned her shirt, and used his trauma shears to cut away her long-sleeved tee.

"Sorry," he whispered, feeling like a voyeur as he positioned monitor leads around her sports bra. The entrance wound was just below her bra, so he was able to avoid that embarrassment, although he would not have hesitated to strip her naked if that was what it took to treat her.

He slapped a plastic-wrapped four-by-four over the entrance wound. She held it in place herself. There was minimal bleeding—not unusual with a GSW from a distance. Contrary to what TV and movies showed, most people didn't gush blood from an entrance wound, not unless a large vein was hit. They also didn't drop dead instantly. A fact that reminded him to stay calm, just breathe.

"Second rule," she gasped, placing her free hand over his.

"Second rule of trauma," he intoned. "Take your own pulse." Meaning if he panicked, he'd be more likely to do more harm than good. "Let's both just take it easy. Slow and steady. Breathe in, breathe out."

She managed a weak smile, and they both took deep breaths. She winced as she exhaled, reminding him to get to work. He grabbed his stethoscope, listened to her breathing.

"Breath sounds still equal," he told her.

"Trachea?" she asked, wincing again as she took another breath. Was it only pain, or was air beginning to accumulate, ready to collapse her lung with a pneumothorax?

"Midline. No JVD."

She nodded. Sweat had broken out on her forehead and she was trembling. Shock.

"I'll start an IV," he told her.

"No. Check. Exit." Her teeth were chattering, preventing her from finishing a sentence. At least he hoped that was all it was. He glanced at the monitor. Heart rate high—to be expected, but blood pressure and pulse ox were okay. For now, at least.

"This is gonna hurt," he told her as he took her shoulders to lean her forward and check for an exit wound. Nothing. He let her lie back. "No exit wound."

"Shit," she gasped. "Get. Seal."

He was already one step ahead, ripping open a sterile package, revealing the clear, adhesive chest seal.

"Make. Sure—"

"Shut up, Alyssa. Used enough of these while in the shitshow. I could do it in my sleep," Blake snapped, wishing she'd conserve her energy.

"Boss." She aimed a thumb at herself.

"If you think I give a fuck about my license right now, I need to check you for brain trauma," he said as he positioned the seal over the wound, pressing down firmly around the edges.

"Jesus!"

The valve in the center fluttered as Alyssa exhaled, releasing the trapped air. With each breath, Blake watched, checking if the seal would hold. All good. But he'd seen guys with similar injuries go downhill fast.

"How's your belly?" He palpated it, hoping the bullet's trajectory hadn't sent it into her liver or kidney. But she had no guarding or rebound tenderness. That was good. He wrapped two emergency blankets around her as he debated: take the time to start an IV here—he was nowhere near as fast and slick as Alyssa was, but he could manage it—or hit the road and get to Potsdam as fast as possible.

"Go," she ordered, making the decision for him. "BP's stable. Gas pedal—"

"Is sometimes the best medicine," he finished for her. Trauma patients had a much better chance at living when they arrived at a trauma center quickly. They used to say within the "golden hour," but in reality, even sooner was best.

He checked to make sure both Alyssa and Thomas were strapped in. Thomas appeared shaken and worried, but otherwise fine. Blake moved to the front seat, keying the radio as he fastened his seatbelt, but it was still on the fritz. He searched his pockets for his cell—gone, probably vanished in the snow while he was dealing with the impostor cop. Shit.

Alyssa's had been in her hand… He fished around under the driver's seat and found it. But the screen was cracked, and there was no life behind it. Well and truly dead.

"I've got no comms," he called to Alyssa as he drove to the strip mall's exit. The storm had worsened, visibility was less than shit. He put the turn signal on and squinted to make sure there was no traffic. "Next stop, Potsdam."

"Hey," Thomas said. "Wasn't the shootout between us and Potsdam? How do we know there's no more of those guys between us and there?"

Blake stopped. He had been so immersed in treating Alyssa that he hadn't thought about what was staring right at him. He turned to face them both.

"That county SUV, driving like a bat out of hell. It wasn't headed to Potsdam, was it?" Real cops would know Eastfork wasn't the right destination for serious injuries.

Real cops would have left someone at the shootout and not just abandoned a crime scene.

"No," Alyssa said. "Eastfork." She twisted to meet his gaze. "We gotta go. Eastfork. Now."

She knew as well as Blake that meant potentially delaying her care if she needed more than what Sara could do with the basic equipment available in the Minor Care clinic.

But then she voiced what he'd been worrying about. "Maybe not cops."

"One guy didn't kill all those officers," he filled in the blanks, then glanced at Thomas.

Alyssa shrugged, leaving the decision—for once—to Blake. Helluva time to give up being the boss.

"Thomas, you get a vote. Eastfork or Potsdam?"

"If Dr. Sara's in trouble along with the rest of the folks at the clinic, hell yeah, we gotta go. What're you waiting for, hit the gas!"

Blake's foot was on the accelerator before the old man finished talking. Sara was in danger, his gut was certain. She and her staff didn't stand any chance against gunmen who had just taken out half a dozen cops.

These guys were dangerous.

Very dangerous.

And they had a serious head start on Blake.

Chapter Fourteen

FRIDAY, February 13th, 8:51 P.M.

BRICK JOINED TYSON in the waiting room, now crowded with patients, family, and the few staff left alive. No one appeared to be a threat, all cowed and cowering. Good.

"What's going on? What's the plan?" Tyson asked in a low voice.

"Harper's coming to give you a hand. Meantime, I have a little job for that one." He jerked his chin at the dispatcher, Wayne. "C'mon, Wayne. I need you to help me with a little communications issue."

The man climbed to his feet, wavering. "Me?"

"Yeah, you run the dispatch office, right? C'mon, show me how it all works, then I'll bring you right back."

"Uh, sure, all right." Not like the guy had any choice, not with Brick's weapon aimed right at him.

Brick smiled, took the guy's arm, and shoved him ahead of him into the hall leading back to the ambulance garage and EMS office.

98

"So, this is where all the action happens, huh?" Brick said, taking in the monitors, radio, and telephone.

"Yeah, pretty much," the guy said, eyeing him curiously.

"Walk me through your comms. There been any outgoing calls since we arrived?"

Wayne shook his head. "How could there be? We were all with you guys."

"Right." Brick brushed the radio controls. "These go to…?"

"Depends on the frequency. EMS and fire, of course. Plus, Potsdam PD, county sheriff, staties. Used to have our own police force here, but they closed it down. Couldn't afford the insurance. Same reason why we're next on the chopping block."

The guy was warming up to Brick, liked to talk about his work, proud of it. Good. Brick could use that. He motioned for Wayne to take his seat. Once he was settled in, the dispatcher visibly relaxed. Very good.

"How come no one's talking on the radios now?" Brick asked.

Wayne messed with the dials, releasing only static. "The storm. Radios have been on the fritz all night."

Brick's eyes narrowed. "What about landlines? Cell phones?"

"Sure, a landline's essential." Wayne chuckled nervously. "Cell reception's spotty at best, especially in this weather." He pulled out his mobile phone, glanced at it, and mumbled, "Zero bars right now."

Brick took the cell and pocketed it. He scanned the tiny room, noting cameras, computers, anything that could jeopardize their operation. "Any other ways to contact the outside? Emergency backup systems?"

"No, sorry."

Brick crouched down, eye level with the man. He stared at him for long moments, noting the sweat gathering, the way his eyes blinked faster…

"You're lying."

Wayne's gaze flicked to the radio.

Brick stood, tapped the radio with his rifle. "Tell me more about the radio, Wayne. What have you heard about us?"

Wayne squirmed, kept his gaze focused on his desk. "There was a report of a state trooper pursuing a robbery suspect. But I didn't hear anything after that from them."

"From them," Brick pushed. "What about from anyone else?"

"Uh, I think, maybe one of our EMS units saw you guys driving here? Called to warn us we might have a trauma coming in, but that was right when you got here, so there wasn't anything we could do." The words poured out of him in a gush. Finally, the truth.

"That's good work, Wayne. I can tell you're a man who likes to stay on top of things. I appreciate that. Most folks just clock in, clock out, don't give a shit. But not you." Brick lowered his head, speaking directly into Wayne's ear. "I think I can trust you, Wayne. Trust you with the one chance you have to save all your friends and those innocent patients in the waiting room. What do you say, ready to be a hero?"

Wayne nodded furiously. "What do I need to do?"

"Just your job, Wayne. Get on the radio and tell them it's all clear here. The ambulance crew thought we were coming here, but they called back to say they got it wrong, we were headed in the other direction to——"

"Potsdam," he supplied eagerly. "That's where cops would go if someone was shot."

"Good, that's good." He nudged him with the butt of

his rifle. "Okay, tell them just like that." Wayne reached for the radio handset, but Brick pressed the rifle butt down on his hand, pinning him to the desk. "Think, Wayne. Would they expect you to call on the landline or radio? After all, it's not an emergency, just passing on information."

"Landline." Brick nodded permission. Wayne's fingers shook as he raised the handset and dialed. Brick tapped the speaker button.

"Dispatch, what's up, Wayne?" came a man's voice.

"Hey, Neil. Just wanted to give you a heads-up. Our medics called back, that SUV with your possible injured officer was headed to Potsdam, not here. Wanted to clarify so you didn't waste units sending them our way."

There was a brief pause that had Brick worried, but then the dispatcher came back with, "Potsdam, right? Forwarding the info now." The sound of typing came over the line. "Did they say which road?"

"Route 37," Wayne said. "I'll let you go now. Sure you guys are swamped with the storm and all."

"Yeah, you're lucky the clinic's about to close for the night. Be safe headed home, the roads are slick as shit."

"Thanks."

Brick hung up the phone for him—sounded like these two were about to exchange cookie recipes or the like. He'd noted the clinic hours from a sign in the waiting room—so no attempt at a secret message or some such shit there. "Good job, Wayne. One last thing. The clinic's supposed to close in a few minutes. Do you have a routine for that? Like call all the ambulances in or alert anyone, set an alarm that a security company is expecting to see activated?"

Wayne shook his head vehemently. "They just lock the doors and turn out the lights. I mean, there's an alarm. There's still valuable stuff in the building. But it gets set by the security guard when his shift is done, and that isn't until midnight."

Brick frowned at the man. Hard enough to make him squirm. "And?"

"Oh, the EMS side of things? My shift also ends at nine when the clinic closes. Used to be when we had an ER here, someone came to relieve me, but now all the calls just go through the county. So, I just lock up and leave, too."

"But there's an ambulance out."

"The medics have their own key codes, come and go when they need. Won't be for long, we're closing down in a few weeks. They're trying to get the ambulance and all the gear donated to the volunteer fire department here in East-fork, but—"

Damn, this guy loved to talk about his job. But Brick had heard more than enough. While Wayne was prattling, Brick shifted position to stand behind Wayne, drew his pistol from its holster, and put two in the back of the man's head.

The gunshots were like sonic booms in the tiny room, rattling the windows. Brick's ears rang, so he felt more than heard steps thudding across the concrete floor of the ambulance bay, raised his gun as the door to the dispatch office was jerked open, only to see Leon standing there.

"What the fuck, man!" Leon was shouting when Brick's hearing cleared. "Give a guy a bit of warning, why don't you?"

Brick had totally forgotten about Leon, assigned to stay outside with the SUV and watch for any cops heading their way.

"Guy was a loser," Brick said, nudging Wayne's body to the side as he ripped the landline from the wall and used his rifle to smash the radio. Leon joined in, enthusiastically destroying the other communication equipment.

After, Leon grinned back at him, inhaled a lungful of smoke from the cigarette he held, then crushed the butt in the ground. "Thought we were undercover as cops."

"Already blew our cover, shot a guard." Brick jerked a thumb at the building interior. "Boss wants you to go help Tyson. He's got a bunch of hostages in the waiting room, needs them guarded." He considered the other man, remembered Leon's propensity for unnecessary violence. "Needs them safe and sound," he clarified. "We might need them for bargaining chips."

Leon side-eyed the doorway and nodded slowly. "Yeah, but we all know Connor's a goner." He grinned at his sick rhyme. "Why don't we just grab the rubies, get the hell outta Dodge?"

Exactly Brick's plan—only not including Leon. "Mercer's got the rubies stashed. Until we know where, he's the boss."

"The temporary boss, you mean." Leon winked. "So, keep the hostages alive until we find the gems and can blow this joint? No witnesses left alive, right?"

"No witnesses," Brick agreed. He just omitted the tiny fact that in his mind, Leon was also a witness, already good as dead along with everyone else in the building.

Chapter Fifteen

FRIDAY, February 13th, 8:53 P.M.

THE AMBULANCE ROARED through Eastfork as fast as Blake could safely drive in the harsh conditions with the wind and snow rushing in through the smashed windshield.

Blake shuddered at the cold as he passed the familiar boarded-up stores and, of course, no pay phones in sight for him to call in the emergency. Whose damned idea was it to take away all the pay phones and landlines anyway?

"How's Alyssa back there?" Blake asked, loud enough for Thomas to hear.

"Stable, I think," he rasped in reply.

"Fine," came her voice, sounding refreshingly annoyed. If she had enough energy to be pissed at him and the situation, he'd take that as a good sign.

"Shout if there's any change, okay?"

"Roger." Thomas sounded as if he was enjoying the ride. Sometimes, adrenaline did that.

As Blake turned into the hospital drive, he flicked

off the lights and slowed, inching along slower than he could've walked it. When he saw the ambulance bay, doors open and lights on, he stopped and idled the engine. Between the snow and the bushes that lined the drive, their ambulance was fairly obscured, he hoped.

The county SUV had been parked haphazardly in the bay, lights still blazing with one of the passenger doors open. An armed man lounged against its hood, smoking a cigarette.

Then two flashes lit up the dispatch window. Blake was too far away to hear any gunshots over the howling wind, but he was reasonably certain those were muzzle flashes from a pistol. The man in the ambulance bay also reacted, raising his rifle and racing to the EMS office, yanking the door open.

Blake watched as a second man appeared in the office window. He was a big guy with a mohawk, also dressed in tactical gear.

"Everything okay?" Alyssa asked.

"I think Wayne may just have been shot," Blake said as he moved to the back of the ambulance.

"Oh, Jesus, no." Thomas stared up at Blake, ashen-faced. "Are you sure?"

"Not one hundred per cent, but close."

"So, those really aren't cops?" Thomas whispered. "What're we gonna do?"

"Not we," Alyssa put in. "Blake, we need to call the cops."

"From our last comms, they should already have folks on the way."

"Twenty minutes, they said. To where the shootout was."

Shit. That was a helluva long time when desperate

armed men were involved. "Are they sending anyone here?"

A shrug was her only answer.

"Here's the plan," he told them. "I'm going to get you guys somewhere safe. Then I'm going in to find a landline, call for back up." Maybe draw the gunmen away from the civilians, he didn't add.

"Old outpatient clinic," Alyssa said.

"Good, that will work."

Far enough from the ER that no one would hear them, safe from the elements and the last place the gunmen would go. Except the former clinic had already been stripped clean, had no power or oxygen.

Blake checked his supply of oxygen canisters. One more beyond what Thomas had. The ambulance had its own supply, but once away from it, both Alyssa and Thomas would need oxygen, and two tanks might not be enough if help was delayed. But there was plenty of O2 in the ambulance bay, and he had to retrieve it.

Weapons. He needed weapons to make the next part work.

Blake had his multitool, a folding knife, and trauma scissors, but they'd only be useful for extremely close quarters fighting. He grabbed the vehicle's toolbox. Inside were a wrench, various screwdrivers, a hammer, and numerous other tools. He chose a Halligan—an eighteen-inch firefighter entry tool with a pry bar at one end and a combo adze and pick at the other. He hefted it in his hands. It felt good—his old M4 carbine would've been better, but at least he didn't feel quite as naked.

"Where are you going with that?" Alyssa asked. He liked that she could breathe easier with the pneumoseal, but knew it was just a temporary fix. One problem at a time, he told himself.

"Gonna shop for supplies. Leave the motor running. I'll be right back."

"Be careful."

He nodded and slipped out of the vehicle. The snow and wind made for decent camouflage, but he took no chances, moving slowly and silently along the shrubs that lined the drive. By the time he reached the EMS bay, both men had vanished. Gone. But for how long?

Blake crossed the parking lot in a low sprint, edging along the wall that led to the bay. He stopped and listened every few yards until he was crouched alongside the SUV.

There was blood smeared on the floor near the SUV. He glanced inside to the rear seat. One of them was injured—pretty badly, based on the amount of blood.

Using the vehicle for cover, he crossed to the dispatch office window and craned his head to look inside. Wayne was dead. All the gear smashed to bits, the landline ripped from the wall. Cell phone? No, the gunmen would've grabbed phones from the hostages first thing.

Back to his original plan, then. He turned to the racks of equipment along the side wall. A wheeled cart held four oxygen tanks. He debated taking the entire cart but worried it might be missed.

He grabbed a trauma bag to augment what he had in the ambulance and slung it over his shoulder. Then he filled his arms with two O2 canisters, fighting to juggle them and the Halligan without any clanging, hating that it took both hands, making him feel vulnerable.

Hurrying out of the bay where the lights made him an easy target, he'd just made it to the exterior wall when the door from the ER opened. Flattening himself against the brick wall, he inched as far into the shadows as possible, giving him an oblique sightline into the bay.

The man with the mohawk walked over to the parked

SUV, searched inside each of the three compartments: front, rear, cargo. Then the guy slammed the door shut, locked the vehicle with a key fob, and leaned against the hood, lighting a cigarette as he looked around.

Blake held his breath. Would he notice the missing oxygen tanks? What was he looking for inside the SUV he and his partners had arrived in?

He contemplated taking the guy out, or maybe using his gear as a cover for infiltrating the ER. But that option had too many risks.

Mohawk crushed his half-smoked cigarette into the pavement and turned, facing the half-empty oxygen rack.

Blake tensed.

"Fuck this," Mohawk muttered, turning on his heel to cross back into the ER.

Blake waited a full minute, but the guy didn't return. Blake withdrew to the ambulance where Thomas was doing an excellent job monitoring Alyssa's screens.

"No change," the old man reported as if he were in charge.

Headlights off, counting on the storm to hide their movement, Blake drove around the building to the old clinic on the far side of the ER, backing up to a plywood-covered door secured with a padlock.

Blake switched off the engine and jumped out, grabbing a Maglite and the Halligan, which made short work of the lock just as it was designed to do. It was fast becoming Blake's favorite tool.

He eased the door open to peek at the gloomy space within. The abandoned clinic wing had been empty for months, but it would suit his needs—for a while at least. He slipped inside, using the Maglite to navigate. There was no equipment left, only worthless trash: a couple of plastic chairs, some stray rolls of toilet paper and bundles of paper towels, a cracked empty red sharps disposal bin, an old wheelchair. The hall parallel to the clinic held a series of interconnected, partially demolished offices that would be even more useless.

Satisfied there were no gunmen or threats waiting, Blake returned to the ambulance. He prepped Alyssa for transport first, hanging the monitor on the gurney railing, piling up the trauma gear, IV bags, and oxygen tanks on her lap and between her legs.

Wrestling the gurney out of the ambulance took more work than he'd anticipated—it wasn't designed for one person to extract while a patient was on board. But with a little huffing, he made it, although Alyssa obviously bore the brunt of his jostling, unable to silence her yelp of pain when the back wheels bounced onto the ground.

"Sorry," he whispered, but she just shook her head and pointed to the door. "Yes, my queen, right away, oh supreme medic."

She managed a weak smile but didn't answer him, which was a bit worrying.

He got her inside, parking the gurney in the empty examination room closest to the exit, just in case they had to make a run for it. Once he had her on oxygen, monitor, and with trauma bags parked on the counter where she could reach them, he returned for Thomas.

Despite not being able to see—or maybe that was an advantage in the darkness—the older man had gathered up his IV bag and tubing, holding it on his shoulder like a pro, his other hand gripping his oxygen tank. At least he hadn't risked climbing down from the ambulance on his own, Blake thought as he helped him to the ground. He hopped back up into the ambulance, grabbing a box of emergency blankets—the clinic wasn't much warmer than the ambulance—three more Maglites, and any meds he imagined Thomas might need to supplement the supply in the med kit.

There wasn't any medication that might help Alyssa. If she got worse, she'd need a chest tube, maybe a blood transfusion, a surgeon and an OR. None of which he had to offer.

He took Thomas into the exam room, parking him on a chair and hanging his IV from a stand he found among the debris in the hall. One wheel was broken, but it worked just fine for his purposes. Setting up a Maglite as a makeshift lantern, he checked Thomas's sugar and electrolytes. The sugar was stable but the potassium was creeping up; the old man needed his dialysis. Soon.

Then he turned to Alyssa. She already had IV supplies spread out over the blanket covering her lap and held her arm out to him. "Easy stick."

"Easy for you to say." He threw a tourniquet around her arm and she pumped her fist, making the veins in her antecubital fossa pop. She was right, she was an easy stick —that and he had a good teacher. He hung her IV on the pole at the head of the bed, then listened to her lungs. "Down a little on the right."

She nodded. Of course, she'd know if her own breathing changed. He checked the chest seal. It wasn't fluttering.

"Blood clot. I'm going to swap it out." He grabbed a new seal from the trauma kit and reapplied, relieved when the valves began to move as she exhaled. But the fact that the first one had clogged so quickly made him worry she might be bleeding into the area around her lung. But her vitals were okay—not great, but okay.

"We've got two more seals." He placed them where she could reach them, beside the other supplies. He looked around. There wasn't anything more he could do to help them.

"Go," Alyssa said.

"Yeah, don't let them hurt anyone else," Thomas chimed in.

"Hey." Alyssa grabbed Blake's arm. "First rule."

He nodded grimly. "I won't do anyone any good if I get killed."

"Yeah, cuz we'd be truly screwed then," Thomas added.

Blake rummaged through the trauma bag, grabbed a roll of duct tape, smashed it flat, and slid it into his inside jacket pocket where he kept his good luck charm: his grandfather's old Zippo lighter that had never failed to light. Not even during his Afghan tour.

Wasn't much else that might be handy when dealing with enemy combatants—scalpels were too flimsy as weapons, and IV tubing was too pliable to be good for anything other than a garrote. If Blake was close enough to use a garrote, he could just as easy choke a man out himself. Ranger School might have been years ago, but those skills were deeply ingrained.

He moved his Kershaw Drivetrain folding knife from his belt to his sock, sliding it out of sight inside his boot. The Maglite, he attached to his belt alongside his multitool. He grabbed his Halligan, turned one last time to Thomas and Alyssa, their faces ghostly white in the other Maglite's LED.

"Good luck," Thomas said.

Alyssa waved him off. "Later, gator."

He stepped outside into the corridor. Within a few steps, he was plunged into darkness.

Chapter Sixteen

Friday, February 13th, 9:01 P.M.

DESPITE THE PRESSURE dressing and IV fluids, Connor's vitals weren't stabilizing. Sara wrapped the fingers of one hand around his radial pulse, pressed her other hand against his neck. Shit, shit, shit. He needed so much more than she could offer him.

"Not good, is it, Doc?" he murmured, eyes watching her every move.

"Could be better," she admitted.

Two shots sounded. Loud enough that the shooter had to be close by.

Kelly dropped the IV bag she'd been replacing and spun toward the sound.

Sara touched the nurse's arm, steered her away from the door toward the tall cupboard in the farthest corner of the room. "Why don't you check the equipment closet, see if you can find anything helpful?"

Kelly was trembling beneath Sara's hands. But then she

gathered herself and walked over to the closet, with only a quick, fearful glance as she passed by the doorway.

"Nick, give Connor another bolus," Sara instructed her PA. Despite her own fear, she strode to the doorway, stepped over Luca's blood, and went to find Mercer.

He was across the hall, leaning against the wall, smoking a damn cigarette.

"Who did you kill this time?" she demanded.

"How's my brother?"

"Stable. For now. But—"

He shook his head at her, an eyebrow raised, daring her to finish that sentence.

Sara choked back the truth. "He's fine."

"Better be."

The door from the ambulance bay opened and Mohawk Guy—Brick—along with another of Mercer's men emerged. Mercer flicked his cigarette ash. "All good?"

"Communication problem taken care of, boss," Brick said, giving Sara a sidelong look.

"Good. Leon, check on the hostages. Brick, get in there." He nodded to the treatment room. "Keep an eye on Connor."

The two men left.

Sara pulled both fists into her belly, pressing hard. It was the only way to keep from lashing out. "Wayne," she gasped. "You killed Wayne. Why?"

Mercer stepped forward, his hand holding the cigarette raised close enough that she felt its heat on the skin below her eye. It took everything she had to hold her ground. "Anyone not working to save my brother's life is expendable. So, maybe you best get back to work, Doctor." He spat out her title as if it was a curse. "Now!"

Sara stared at him. The cigarette edged closer to her

face. "No. Not until you promise no one else dies. I'm responsible for these people."

He flicked the cigarette away, but she had the distinct impression that he would've preferred to grind it into her eye. The only reason he hadn't was that he needed her. That was her only leverage.

"I think you have it wrong, Doc," he said. "I'm responsible for who lives and dies. Don't you forget it."

Sara played the only card she had in an all-or-nothing gamble. After all, he'd kill them all as soon as Connor was dead—or even, if by some miracle, Sara did save him. Mercer wouldn't leave any witnesses alive. "If you want us to keep helping your brother, I need assurances—"

He held up a hand. "I like you, Doc. You play hardball, just like me. Okay. Your people are safe. Their lives are in your hands. Now, go. Save my brother."

Sara jerked her chin in a nod, sealing their devil's bargain. Then she returned to her patient.

When she re-entered the trauma bay, she saw that the guy with the mohawk, Brick, actually didn't seem very interested in what they were doing for Connor—that, or he was more squeamish than his appearance suggested. He was in the corner where Connor's clothing and gear, along with Luca's body lay, sorting through Connor's stuff.

She turned her back to him and joined Nick and Kelly at Connor's beside.

"No improvement," Nick murmured.

Sara agreed. If anything, Connor was worse, his BP dropping as he slipped further into shock.

"Are they gonna kill everyone? I think they might kill everybody," Kelly blurted.

"Try not to think about it. Take a breath," Sara said. "Focus on Connor. Hypovolemic shock, but we have nothing to transfuse." Stating the problem out loud always helped get the team back in sync. "I'm gonna need to open him up, find where the bleeding's coming from. But I can't—"

"Without pain control," Nick finished for her. "Think we might have that covered. Sorta."

Kelly turned to the head of the bed. "I found the old nitrous set up in the equipment closet, behind some backboards. Not sure if it still works."

"No, no, that's a good start," Sara told them. "Nick, get it set up—fifty/fifty mix of O2 to nitrous oxide. Kelly, mix me an epi drip and get it started at a mic a minute."

They turned to their jobs, seemed relieved to have something to keep their minds off the world beyond their patient.

Sara moved to Connor's head. "Nick's going to switch your oxygen mask for nitrous oxide—"

"Laughing gas?" he asked.

"Exactly. I need to remove the dressing and explore your wound. I don't have any pain meds, and I don't want to try to knock you out for intubation." She could have figured out a possible combo of meds from the crash cart or even paralyze him without sedation—the very definition of cruelty, since the patient would feel all the pain, but be trapped inside their own body, unable to move. But she knew there was no way Mercer would allow her to render Connor unconscious. Who knew how many of her people would end up dead if she tried?

"It's okay, Doc." His tone was so trusting that Sara felt guilty for even contemplating what she was about to do in these primitive conditions.

"It's still going to hurt," she warned him. "But maybe you won't care as much."

"I'm good. Do what you need."

She glanced at the nearby IV stand where Kelly was

hanging the epi drip. Epinephrine was pure adrenaline, it could buy them time, but it wasn't the answer to Connor's problems. For that, he needed blood and an operating room and to go back in time.

But it would create the illusion that he was stable. Hopefully, enough to convince Mercer.

Sooner rather than later, Connor was going to die, she was pretty sure. She wanted to save him, she wished she could save him. As her patient, he belonged to her as much as he did to Mercer.

But deep down, she knew better. The best she could hope for was that by prolonging Connor's suffering—and life—she was giving everyone else a chance to live.

Chapter Seventeen

FRIDAY, February 13th, 9:11 P.M.

BLAKE STEALTHILY MOVED along the corridor of the abandoned part of the building, Halligan in hand. He stopped occasionally to listen, attempting to gauge where in the building everyone might be. It was likely the hostages would be gathered in the waiting room, the only place large enough to hold several people plus staff.

He assumed there were between four and six gunmen based on the size of the SUV that had brought them here. At least one of them was injured, from the blood he'd seen on the ambulance bay floor. So, count on five. If it was him, he'd want at least two with the hostages—one man was too easy to rush and overwhelm. That left three patrolling or with their injured comrade.

He stopped at the double doors dividing the old clinic wing from the emergency department. They used to be locked, requiring a keycode to access the ER, but since the demolition work had begun, they were left unsecured.

Light shone through the doors' narrow windows, but he didn't see any movement. The waiting room was at the far end of the corridor. The nearest treatment rooms to this entrance were the trauma bay and the suture and ortho rooms. He edged one door open a crack and listened.

A woman's voice. Sara. Talking to a man outside the trauma bay. She was angry—furious. He couldn't make out their words, but that didn't stop relief from washing over him.

Sara was alive.

That didn't mean she was unharmed, though, he thought as relief turned to fury, burning deep in his belly, energizing him. He was desperate to charge down the hall, save her despite having no idea what kind of resistance he'd face.

No. Wrong.

He knew these men were well-armed, so any foolish efforts to rescue Sara or any of the hostages could just as easily get innocents killed. Including Blake.

And then who would save Sara? *First rule of trauma,* he heard Alyssa's voice in his head. Why was she always right?

If he followed the corridor past the trauma room and ambulance entrance, he'd reach the main reception area. But his first priority was to find a phone, call for backup. The nurses' station was at the center of the square of hallways that made up the ER wing, out of sight of both the waiting room and trauma bay. And he knew it had working phones.

He circled through the rear hallway, coming out at the nurse's station: a glass-walled report room, med room, supply closet, and large charting desk, it was the heart of the ER.

And it was blissfully empty.

He ducked down behind the desk, taking the landline phone with him and dialed 911.

"Come on, come on," he mouthed silently.

A few seconds passed. The slowest seconds Blake had ever experienced.

"911, what's your emergency?"

When Blake spoke, his voice came out in a harsh whisper. "This is Blake Harrow. I'm at Eastfork ER. There are gunmen here. Hostage takers, maybe four to six of them. Armed with MP5s, handguns, and they have already killed the dispatch operator, possibly others."

The operator's tone immediately shifted. "Stay calm. We have officers close by. They'll be there soon."

"How soon is soon? These guys—they killed at least four cops already. They're desperate and ruthless, a bad combo." Blake wiped sweat from his forehead. "There's no good tactical approach," he added quickly. "They'll see it coming if you come in the front or through the EMS bay."

There was a brief silence. "Understood. Is there another way in?"

Blake swallowed hard, glancing toward the back of the building. "There's a door in the rear—part of the old outpatient clinic wing that's closed down. I left a wounded paramedic, Alyssa Abbasi, and an elderly patient, Thomas Milton, there. They're not known to the gunmen. That might be a good route for law enforcement, but you must be careful. I'm gonna see what I can do from here."

The operator's voice tightened. "Sir, you need to stand down. Hide somewhere safe, and don't engage. I repeat: do not engage with them. It's too dangerous."

"But—" Blake clenched his jaw.

"No. Do nothing. Officers are on route. Just stay out of sight."

Blake heard approaching footsteps and cut the call. He

quickly slid the phone back to the top of the desk. There wasn't room below it for him—and it was a poor tactical position, so he ducked his head up just far enough to see one of the gunmen emerging from a restroom down the hall.

Blake did a quick scuttle to the supply room door on the far wall, out of the gunman's line of sight. He slid inside, holding the door shut. Footsteps approached. Shit. He did a mental inventory of what he remembered being stored inside here. Gauze, splints, tape, bandages, a myriad of miscellaneous medical paraphernalia, none of them potential lethal weapons.

Except… He clicked his light on, found what he wanted along with a bonus treat: a small digital alarm. He quickly programmed it, then switched the Maglite off again as the footsteps grew closer.

Gripping the Halligan in one hand, his new weapon in the other, he pressed his eye to the crack in the door. A man's shadow passed behind the desk.

Now or never, was he going to hide, or seek?

He thought of Sara at the mercy of these monsters.

Seek. Most definitely seek.

Chapter Eighteen

FRIDAY, February 13th, 9:16 P.M.

BLAKE BRUSHED his finger across the small alarm he'd found. The nurses used it to keep track of medication timings, but he only needed a quick ten-second countdown. He tapped the button for it to start and set the alarm back on a shelf, then took two steps back to wait in the dark.

Eight, nine, ten, he counted silently. BEEP, BEEP.

The footsteps hurried close. BEEP, BEEP.

The door knob rattled.

Blake fell into a fighting stance just beyond where the door would swing into the closet. Raised his weapon. Only one chance at this.

The door burst open as if someone had kicked it. Someone had. Leaving his assailant off balance as he rushed the room. Blake didn't hesitate. He ignored the other man's outstretched arm holding the pistol and instead stepped inside to aim his own weapon directly at the man's face.

The aerosol can of liquid nitrogen was used to freeze warts, so it didn't contain a large amount of the gas. But more than enough to freeze a man's corneas, blinding him.

The man screamed, arms flailing trying to block Blake, but Blake fended him off with the Halligan. The heavy tool was unwieldy to swing in such tight quarters, but right now Blake didn't need to actually use it to do much damage, just keep the man from twisting his gun hand around to aim at Blake's back or legs.

The man seemed to have forgotten he even had a gun, letting it fall as his dominant hand flew back to protect his eyes. Too late, as ice already crusted his eyelids and covered his eyes like thick frost. His shrieks of pain became shrill— the one flaw in Blake's plan.

Blake kept his hand on the nozzle until the can sputtered, emptied. Then he spun the man into the closet, jammed the Halligan crowbar first into his belly to drive him back, and slammed the door shut to muffle the man's cries. He could still hear the supplies crashing to the ground as the man heaved his body around.

One more flaw to his plan—the door didn't lock. Blake grabbed a notepad from the desk, folded it in two, and wedged it into the bottom of the door. It wouldn't last long, but long enough for Blake to leave. He just wished he'd been able to grab the man's pistol or rifle.

"Tyson? Where are you, mate?" A voice with a South African lilt came from farther down the hallway, followed by hurried footsteps that echoed ominously against the linoleum floor.

Blake was out of time. He braced himself against the wall the South African would need to turn around to reach the supply closet where his comrade, Tyson, was hammering on the door. It'd only give him a split second of advantage, but he'd take what he could get.

The South African whipped around the corner. "Tyson, what—"

Blake swung the Halligan against the gunman's back with a hard whack. The impact sent the man stumbling against the desk. Then, in one fluid motion, Blake lunged forward and aimed a second strike against the man's gun hand.

The man was fast and well-trained. He anticipated the blow and instead of blocking it, he used Blake's momentum against him, grabbing the hand holding the Halligan and ducking behind Blake, almost taking his arm out of its socket. But Blake knew that trick and responded by stepping into the hold, removing the man's leverage, then used his free hand to try to pry the pistol away from the other man.

For an instant, their eyes locked as they performed their macabre choreography. The South African flashed a smile as if he was finally having fun. He let his pistol fall to the ground—better than it being captured by Blake—and brought Blake's wrist down against the edge of the desk. The sudden shock of pain numbed Blake's hand and the Halligan flew free, skidding across the space.

With his hand out of commission, hopefully only temporarily, Blake drove his knee hard into the man's midsection, knocking the wind from him and leaving him gasping for air. As the gunman doubled over, desperately trying to recover, Blake followed up by slamming his elbow into the base of the man's neck—the blow connected with a nasty thud, sending the gunman crashing to the ground.

Taking no chances, Blake threw his body onto the gunman's back to finish the job. The assailant rolled violently, desperately trying to shake Blake off, twisting his body around to deliver a swift elbow jab to Blake's ribs.

Blake cried out as the electric shock of pain felt like it jolted through every one of his bones. The South African tried to have another crack at Blake's ribs, but Blake, gritting his teeth, grabbed the back of the gunman's collar, yanked him back down, and, with a controlled but forceful motion, slammed the gunman's head into the floor.

Dazed and disoriented, the gunman struggled, but Blake's resolve was stronger. Then a noise somewhere along the corridor stopped him in his tracks.

More of them were coming.

He needed to stay alive, not get caught now. Otherwise, it was over.

Leaving these chumps alive was not ideal at all, but there was no time.

Blake jumped up, retrieved the South African's pistol from the floor, and raced down the hall, back the way he'd come.

He slipped through the doorway and along the darken corridor, disappearing into the abandoned wing. When he didn't hear anyone following, he cracked the door open just enough to hear two quick gun shots.

"Harper, what the hell?"

"Idiot was no good to us blind," the South African said.

He'd just executed one of his partners, Blake realized. Which meant these men wouldn't think twice about killing the hostages.

Chapter Nineteen

FRIDAY, February 13th, 9:16 P.M.

EVAN HAD NEVER SEEN his mom cry like this before. Silent, choking sobs that moved down her throat without a sound or tear escaping. Her grip on his hand was so tight, his fingers had gone numb.

Pretty much everything was numb except the stupid big toe that still throbbed like crazy. He wished the lady doctor would come back. She seemed like she could handle anything, knew all the answers. Made him feel…safe.

But right now, he and everyone else were anything but safe.

They'd been herded by a big, scary guy with an equally scary looking army-style rifle into the waiting area. There was Evan and his mom, a lady with a splint on her arm and her husband, the clerk who'd signed them in, a guy with a wispy beard and his hand wrapped in a bloody towel, and a lady in one of those special aprons his dentist's assistant used when they took x-rays.

There had been another guy as well, an old guy with a fat belly, but two more men with guns had come and one of them had taken him away, leaving two men to guard them. One of them had ransacked the clerk's desk, said he was looking for gaffer tape.

Evan wasn't sure what he meant, but he didn't think he meant the kind of tape Evan used on his hockey stick or that his mom used to wrap presents.

And then there was the gunfire. Everything had happened so fast, Evan hadn't even had time to think about what that meant until now, when the men with guns retreated to the doorway, leaving the hostages with space to think.

Thinking was the last thing Evan wanted to do. He wasn't supposed to play video games rated T or M, but their goalie's big brother let them when the team had sleepovers at his house. All that blood. And other stuff.

The gunshots had come twice, once before and once after the old man got taken away. So, was he dead? Evan bet he was dead. Wouldn't give up the code to a safe or something. And maybe someone before him. Which meant any one of them could be next.

He couldn't help it, his foot started tapping so hard that his entire leg was bouncing. And he had to pee, so bad.

Then the guy with the beard tapped his arm. "Is it Evan?" He kept his voice low. The two guards were gabbing, not paying any attention anyway. "I'm Tony. What team you play for?"

Evan had to think twice. His brain was drowning in visions of blood, sounds of gunshots. It took a moment to swim back to here and now. "The Eastfork Icers."

"I always followed the Connecticut Roughriders, since I was born over that way. What about yourself, Evan?"

Normally, Evan wouldn't dream of talking about

anything, even hockey, with a creepy stranger, but somehow, right here, right now, it felt right. Like it made the men with guns seem like they were far, far away. "Yeah, they're good. I'm all in with the Carolina Hurricanes. We went to a few games, didn't we, Mom?"

His mom blinked, and suddenly jerked Evan away from the guy as if he was one of…them.

"It's okay, Mom. I was just telling him we saw the Hurricanes play. Right?" He felt like he had to work to keep her attention.

"Yeah. Right." She blinked again, managed a smile that was more scary than her crying had been. "Great games, both of them."

"Great team," Tony added. "Maybe you'll play for them one day, huh?"

Evan glanced at the two men with guns. But it was down to one guy now, the other had left. "Yeah, if we ever get out of here."

His mom and Tony exchanged a glance before Tony leaned closer, lowering his voice to a bare whisper.

"I've been here a few times. I know this place. They may have locked the main doors, but there's a fire exit down the corridor, just go left and we're outta here. Two doors to freedom."

"I'm not sure," Mom replied uncertainly. "What about the guards?"

"One of them just left to go pee. If the other gets distracted, might be our chance. Under one minute, we'll be outside and in the parking lot."

"I don't know," Mom said in the tone that really meant: *that's too dangerous, you're not allowed.*

Evan heard that tone all the time whenever his friends wanted to do something fun like learn skate tricks or jump their bikes.

Mom always put safety first. But maybe this wasn't the best time to play it safe. In the video games, it was always the stupid bystanders doing nothing that got killed first.

He looked at her, meeting her eyes. "Mom, I don't wanna die here. We should get out of here, like he says."

"Too dangerous," Mom whispered.

"But if we stay here, it's dangerous."

"Wasn't trying to upset you," Tony said. "Just wanted you to know the layout in case you get a chance."

A distant beeping, like an alarm clock sounded, caused the second guard to turn away, poke his head through the door. "Tyson?" he shouted. He turned, waved his gun at them. "Stay put." Then he stepped into the hall—heading right, Evan noted. Away from their escape.

Tony jumped up, went to the doorway, and poked his head out, looking both ways. He waved to the rest of the group. "C'mon, it's clear!"

Evan gulped, but squeezed his mom's hand and hauled her to her feet. "Mom, we gotta go, now!"

Tony led the way. They turned left into a long hallway where all the patient rooms were empty, past the room where the doctor had soaked Evan's foot—he still only wore one shoe, the other foot barefoot, he realized—toward a set of double doors.

Then two gunshots sounded from behind them. Evan's mom froze, tugging him to a halt. "We need to go back, before they know we're missing," she said.

"Mom, it's right there—"

The sound of a man's running footsteps, so loud they almost felt like more gunshots. Tony was mere steps from the doors to freedom, Evan and his mom caught between him and the footsteps.

A man pounded around the corner, his rifle aimed. He fired, Evan could feel the bullets scream past him, the sound louder than any thunder he'd ever heard. The shots hit Tony in the back, making his body jerk even as he kept on running, his arms reaching for the doors…until he fell in a heap. And didn't move again.

Evan couldn't hear anything, couldn't see anything beyond the tight circle of light surrounding Tony's body. He stood frozen, knew his mother was screaming and clawing at him, but he couldn't move, not even when the man grabbed him, lifting him off his feet, carrying him like a baby. Pain lanced through Evan—the man's rifle slung across his chest was pressed against Evan's back, and it was hot enough to sting.

That never happened in video games.

And with a rush, Evan's senses returned, and he realized this was all too real.

Chapter Twenty

FRIDAY, *February 13th, 9:16 P.M.*

NOTHING LIKE TRYING to perform a miracle in front of an armed audience, Sara thought.

Both Mercer and Brick stood, watching their every move, as Kelly and Nick prepped Connor for Sara's exploratory surgery.

"This better work, Doc," Mercer warned her.

As if she didn't know the consequences.

"Yeah, he don't look too good," Brick added.

Great, another expert opinion chiming in.

But it was Connor who she concentrated on. Now masked, gloved, and gowned, she peered down at her patient, meeting his eyes. They were glassy, the nitrous doing its job. "You okay, Connor?"

"All good, Doc," he said dreamily.

"Here we go, then." She moved to his belly, Nick across from her and Kelly at her right, ready to supply Sara with whatever she needed.

Sara's hands trembled ever so slightly as she raised her scalpel in one hand, a wad of gauze in the other. She exchanged a glance with Kelly and Nick. Both were pale, fear etched into their faces, but their eyes were steady. They all knew what was at stake here.

If Connor didn't live through this, none of them would.

"Remove the pressure dressing," she ordered.

Nick used a clamp to pull the gauze packing away. Blood—much too thin and watery—oozed from the gunshot wound.

Without hesitation, Sara began her midline incision, her scalpel slicing Connor's skin and subcutaneous tissue from sternum down and around his umbilicus. Then she and Nick separated the wound edges, opening up her surgical field.

"Pack it," she told Kelly as more blood rushed over the edges of the incision, dripping onto the floor. "Nick, retract the bowel." He gathered the loops of intestine in a saline-soaked towel, cradling it to the side where it wouldn't obstruct Sara's view.

Connor gave a low groan that had Mercer tensing. But then Connor relaxed, and so did his older brother.

Sara glanced at the monitor, which confirmed what she already knew: Connor hadn't relaxed because the nitrous was working, rather he'd slipped further into shock and was now unconscious. "Kelly, dial up the epi. Max it out."

Kelly hesitated—not because she was unsure of Sara's orders, she knew, but because she was fighting her training by contaminating one hand to touch the non-sterile IV pump. But she did it. "Done."

Beyond the door came the sound of two gunshots. Everyone froze.

"Focus, people," Sara murmured, despite her own churning fear.

Brick tensed, listening to his radio. "Gonna give the guys a hand in the waiting room," he told Mercer.

"What happened?" Mercer's attention was torn between Connor and whatever was going on outside in the rest of the ER.

"Don't worry about it, boss," Brick said. "I'll call if we need you."

Sara would have given anything for a working suction machine. "Use the towels." The gauze wasn't cutting it. "Pack the lower quadrants, let me get a look at the spleen." A ruptured spleen she could at least do something about: clamp off the hilum vessels and stop the bleed. There was clearly a lot more damage to address—including the perforated bowel leaking the stench of stool—but slowing Connor's blood loss would keep him alive. For now.

She found a subcapsular bleed, but nothing serious. To be on the safe side, she clamped the splenic vessels anyway, then turned her attention to Connor's liver. Nothing there beyond a few tiny bleeds, all easily dealt with, but they didn't account for the ongoing bleeding coming from deeper inside his belly.

"Sponge." Kelly slapped another wad of gauze into Sara's waiting hand.

Sara finally was able to see. "Mesenteric vessels. Shredded."

Nick gasped but covered it with a quick cough.

Mercer sensed something was wrong and stepped forward. "What's going on?"

"The bullet damaged the large blood vessels connected to the intestines," Sara told him, surprised by how steady her voice was. "I'm going to clamp them so the bleeding will stop."

"And then you're done? He'll be okay?"

"And then I'm done." It was no lie. There wasn't anything she could do to save Connor. Kelly handed her a vascular clamp. Sara found an intact section of the artery and clamped it, then the vein as well. At least Conor's blood loss would be slowed.

Mercer's radio squawked. It was Brick.

"Mercer, come in." He did not sound happy. Not at all.

Sara exchanged glances with Nick and Kelly. Who was dead this time?

"Good work, Doc," Mercer said. "Finish up, I'll be back." Holding only his radio, he left, footsteps echoing down the hall.

Sara realized this might be their only chance. "Nick, Kelly," she said. "Get out through the ambulance bay. Go."

Kelly's eyes widened. "We can't just leave you—"

"You have to," Sara snapped, her voice sharp with command. "Get help. Go!"

Nick hesitated, but then Connor's weak voice cut through the tension. "She's right…you gotta get out of here. Run."

The two exchanged glances. Then they both looked at Sara.

"Are you sure?"

Sara glared at them, making the message clear. "That's an order. You guys might be our only hope."

That got their attention. Kelly gave Sara the towel she was holding.

Nick went to the door, looked down the hall. "Coast's clear."

Not even bothering to strip free of their surgical garb, both gave Sara one last look, then ran out, their footsteps quickly fading away.

With the room now eerily quiet, Sara turned back to Connor. His eyes met hers.

"I can't save you," she said softly, her voice trembling slightly. "But *we* can save the hostages."

Connor's gaze didn't waver. "How?"

"If I stop the blood flow to the rest of your body, your heart will pump what's left to your brain, keep you conscious."

"How long?" He hadn't even hesitated. Did he understand that she was talking about killing him?

"Not long. You've already lost too much blood. Maybe ten to fifteen minutes. At most."

He nodded, giving her permission to both condemn him and absolve herself. "Do it."

Breaking every oath she had ever taken as a doctor was a knife twisting in her gut, but there was no other way.

She drew a deep breath, took the clamp from the vascular tray, and gripped it tightly, focusing on the grim task. Carefully, she worked through the blood-soaked packing gauze to isolate the abdominal aorta. She chose the largest vascular clamp, strong enough to hold the blood vessel closed, gentle enough not to rip its walls.

As she worked, Sara couldn't help but think of all the lives she had helped save in this very room. Now she was deliberately ending one.

She locked the clamp into place, sealing his fate.

Connor's gaze remained lucid as the increased blood flow to his brain kept him painfully aware, his breaths coming in shallow gasps.

She replaced his intestines and packed as many towels as she could into his abdominal cavity. Then covered him with a drape. Hiding the evidence.

Backing away from her dirty secret, she stripped free of

her bloody gloves and gown, pulled her mask off so Connor could see her face.

"It's done," she told him. "How are you doing?"

"Better. Don't feel much, just cold."

"Your blood's being replaced with IV fluids, and you're in shock." She hesitated, but she had to give him the option, it was only right. "If things get too bad, I can—"

He shook his head, his oxygen mask slipping. "No. No." Then he whispered, "I never wanted any killing. Never wanted it."

His gaze locked with hers, and despite her shame for what she'd just done, condemning him, failing him, she didn't look away. He deserved that much from her.

"Save them," he ordered her.

"I will," Sara vowed.

Chapter Twenty-One

FRIDAY, February 13th, 9:21 P.M.

BRICK SHOVED the hockey mom and her son back into the waiting room and glowered at all the occupants, following his gaze with his rifle.

"Sit down and shut up. Anyone moves, I'll shoot you dead."

They huddled and cried and kept their gazes down, not daring to look at him. Of course not, he had the power here. He was in charge.

Leon and Harper stumbled into sight from the other direction. Harper looked like he'd been in a barroom brawl.

Brick stepped out so the hostages wouldn't hear. "What the hell happened to you two?"

"Tyson's dead," the South African said. "We got jumped by some guy. Not one of them." He nodded to the hostages in the waiting room. "Guy had a uniform on."

"A cop?" Brick snapped.

"No. He wasn't a cop. Knew how to fight, though." He thought. "A medic, I think."

"You think?"

"He had a crowbar like what firefighters use. So, yeah, medic or fireman."

Brick turned to Leon. "You see the guy?"

"No, he was gone when I got there, didn't see where to."

Idiots. He was working with a bunch of idiots. Never minded that he'd recruited them himself. "Get in there. Secure those hostages."

"With what?" Harper asked. "Couldn't find any gaffer tape."

"It's fuckin' duct tape, and you should have your own." Brick fished the small roll he carried from his inside jacket pocket. Didn't everyone carry duct tape? Shit came in handy all the damn time. "That won't be enough, there'll be more in the ambulance bay or the cop's SUV."

"On it," Leon said, taking off before Brick could give him the tedious task of restraining the hostages.

"Keep an eye out for your fireman," Brick called after him. Then, to Harper, "I'm going to patrol, let Mercer know the situation. Think you can manage here?" It was more a challenge than a question. As far as Brick was concerned, if not for the rubies, he'd kill 'em all and blow this joint now. Shit was getting too fuckin' real.

Brick drew his sidearm and went down the corridor where they said the firefighter had ambushed them. He checked several empty patient rooms until he arrived at a nursing station. There he found an open walk-in closet. Lying on the floor was a man: Tyson.

He'd been shot twice through the back of the head, execution style. Definitely not the work of some rando fireman. Brick rolled him over, cringed at the way his face and eyes were red and swollen—not just the eyelids, but the eyeballs looked swelled up and milky. What the hell had done that?

Leon appeared from the ambulance bay, holding several rolls of duct tape as if he'd just won the lottery. "You were right. I found it!"

"Get back to the waiting room. Help Harper tie everyone up. Then I want you to go on patrol, find the motherfucker who did this." Brick met the other man's gaze, dared him to look away. "Think you can handle that?"

"Don't worry about me, Brick. You know I can. Dude's as good as dead." He did a little celebration dance as if he'd scored a touchdown, then took off running.

Brick watched him leave, shaking his head. He needed to find those damn rubies so he could get the fuck out of Dodge.

Best way to do that was to get Mercer talking. Draw him close, remind him how much he trusted Brick—all the while acting like Mercer was in charge.

Time to call the boss. He keyed his radio. "Mercer, come in."

After a moment, Mercer said, "I'm here, whatcha need, Brick?"

"Tyson and Harper. They got jumped, and now Tyson's dead."

"What the fuck? Who?"

"Harper said the guy looked like a fireman. No sign of him now."

"Where you at?"

"Nurse's station."

"I'm on my way."

Brick didn't have time to do much other than to pat down Tyson's body in the off chance that he had the rubies

—although he was certain Harper and Leon would've already done that. If only he'd seen what had happened to them back at Watts's house.

Mercer arrived, his expression grim.

"How's Connor?" Brick asked.

"Stable. That's what the doc calls it. Ask me, he looks like hell."

"Think she's not doing what she can?"

Mercer ran both palms over his face. "No. That's the problem. I think she is doing everything she can think of." He glanced at Tyson's body. "Maybe we just need to give her more incentive. And flush out this fireman of yours."

He sat down at the desk and picked up the phone, jabbed the button labeled *Intercom*. He spoke and his voice echoed through the empty hallways like the voice of god.

"This is a message to the intruder who just killed my guy. Well, good work. I congratulate you. You're one tough cookie. However, I have no time for games. So…" His voice slowed and deepened. "I'm gonna start killing the hostages, from the youngest to the oldest, until you give yourself up. You got five minutes. Starting now."

Chapter Twenty-Two

FRIDAY, *February 13th, 9:21 P.M.*

THOMAS GRIPPED his mylar blanket tighter, the metallic fabric crinkling noisily. It was so damn cold in here. "Alyssa, did I ever tell you about the time Rose and I stowed away on a luxury yacht?" He smiled at the memory.

Alyssa didn't answer. He rotated the flashlight to aim it at her. Her eyes were closed and she was struggling to breathe. Suddenly, the monitor alarm went off. He jumped up, went to her, tugging his IV so hard he pulled it out. Ignoring the thin stream of blood running down his arm, he tried to focus on the monitor, but it was a blur of green and red and yellow waves.

"Thomas," Alyssa gasped.

He found her hand, grasped it. "I'm here. What do you need?"

"Seal. Clogged." She slapped a hand against the monitor, silencing it.

But when he followed the movement with the flash-light, he realized she was really reaching for the special bandage Blake had already replaced once.

What had Blake done? Thomas tried to remember, but the entire world was like looking through the wrong end of a frosted whiskey tumbler, had been for years now thanks to his diabetes. He'd learned to navigate the world by sticking to familiar routines and by translating the blurry blobs of color and waves of motion into his own version of reality.

Alyssa fumbled at the chest seal, peeling it off. Thomas peered at it. There was no bleeding, but if he remembered what had happened before, that wasn't a good thing. It meant there was blood clotting beneath the bandage that was meant to act like a valve.

"Tell me what to do?" He choked down the sob that felt like a rock in his throat. He hadn't felt this helpless since the cancer ate at Rose while all he could do was sit by and watch her suffer and fade away before his eyes. His damn eyes. They worked too damn well back then and were useless now! "Alyssa, what do you need?"

She sat up, leaning forward, working so hard to breathe that even he could see her neck muscles straining with the effort. But she managed to point to the small tray containing the equipment Blake had used to start her IV. Thomas grabbed it, set it on her lap. Her entire body bobbed up and down with every breath.

"Is this it?"

A nod and her finger inched along the various needles in their packaging. Finally, she stopped on one basin containing three IVs. He took one, held it close to his eyes with the light aimed straight at it. "It says fourteen-gauge angiocatheter. Is this the one?"

Another jerk of her chin, then she grabbed a fistful of

gloves from the larger well beside the alcohol swabs. She thrust them at him, made a cutting motion with her fingers.

"Cut it?"

She held up one finger.

"Cut off a finger?"

Another nod.

He took the medical scissors from the tray, peered at the glove finger, and cut it almost at the palm. While he was working, she'd wiped the area below her collarbone with alcohol and opened the IV catheter. He handed her the glove finger, and to his surprise she slid the needle through the inside of the glove, then leaned back. With a grunt of effort, she jammed the needle into her own ribcage.

"Alyssa!"

She fell back against the bed. Her hand trembled as she fought to remove the needle from the plastic IV tube. He shone the light on it, managed to grab it and slide it free while she held the glove finger and plastic part in place against her skin. As sudden whoosh of air released along with a steady trickle of blood—more blood than his own IV had released when he'd yanked it out.

"You're bleeding? Is that okay?"

The glove's finger closed over the IV's opening as she inhaled. One breath, another.

"Good god, let's not do that again," she mumbled, her eyes closed. But none of those extra muscles were working to help her breathe, and her lips weren't as dusky.

He began to pull the IV tray away, but she hugged it tight.

"If it clots—"

Thomas filled in the blanks. "You might have to do that again."

A sudden wave of nausea hit him, and it had nothing to do with his blood sugar. What a fool he'd been earlier, acting as if this was all some grand adventure for him, a lark. These were his friends, and they might die tonight.

"Blake will be back soon," Thomas muttered, more to himself than to Alyssa. "He'll know what to do." But was Blake coming back? There had been shots from inside the building. It felt like a war was going on.

Alyssa's eyes fluttered open at the sound of his voice. She reached for his hand, but only to redirect the flashlight beam toward the monitor. "Sats still low."

"Maybe your oxygen is running low?" He bent over to look at the gauge on her tank—in the red zone.

"You can use mine," he told her. He'd discarded his own mask a while ago, didn't like the cold air blowing at him or the plastic-like stench of the bottled air. Using the flashlight to guide him, he shuffled back to his side of the room and checked his tank. Then realized when he'd taken it off, he'd left it running, hadn't even tried to shut it off.

Please, he prayed. Just one small miracle, for my friend, please.

Prayers had been useless when Rose was suffering, but he'd try anything. He leaned down, checked the gauge.

Empty.

And he had no idea how to switch with a new tank— the valve needed to come off the old, be inserted on the new, then the tubing hooked up. And he seemed to remember Blake wielding some kind of wrench? Maybe?

"Hang in there, Alyssa," he whispered, his voice trembling with fear and determination. "I'm gonna get you out of here, get you to Potsdam, and get you looked at. Trust me." Thomas felt his heart breaking as he looked down at the young medic who had always been so full of life, joking and singing with him, always a smile and the time to listen to an old man's ramblings.

Now life seemed to be draining right out of her. Just like Rose.

No. Not again. He couldn't face that, watching helpless...

Alyssa tried to smile, but the attempt quickly morphed into a grimace, pain etching deep lines into her usually cheerful features. Her eyes drifted shut once again, but her chest still rose and fell, but he could tell her right side moved differently than her left.

He used the light to survey the dark, abandoned clinic room, turning over options. Memories from his youth flashed before him.

He would drive her in that ambulance himself. It would be a struggle. He hadn't been able to drive for years due to his deteriorating vision. Still, he had to try.

Alyssa's life hung in the balance.

Thomas moved out into the hallway. He scanned the debris—maybe they'd left an oxygen tank that still had some juice? He stumbled forward, trying to focus, almost tripping on a discarded wheelchair with a ripped seat back. Nothing. He was wasting time.

He turned toward the rear door but stopped in his tracks when the intercom spluttered to life. It was difficult to hear the words, as there seemed to be no working speakers on their end of the hallway, but he moved toward the voice, down the corridor until the words became clear.

"...I'm gonna start killing the hostages, from the youngest to the oldest, until you give yourself up."

Thomas dropped his head, leaned against the wall to steady himself, and drew in labored, raspy breaths. That asshole on the mic sounded like he meant what he said.

Killing the youngest to the oldest?

Jesus, what to do?

Blake must have been giving them a run for their money. Must still be if the bad guys were getting that desperate to kill their only bargaining chips. He smiled at that.

Maybe it was time for Thomas to get in on the action. Because he had to admit there was no way in hell he'd be able to get Alyssa to the ambulance, much less drive anywhere, without killing them both. But maybe there was still something left on this Earth for him to do, one last thing…

He'd had a good run, but Rose, God bless her soul, was waiting for him.

Perhaps now was the time. Whatever happened, he didn't fear death. Not now.

Thomas knew what to do.

Chapter Twenty-Three

FRIDAY, February 13th, 9:24 P.M.

As Blake entered the outpatient wing, he worried someone might come after him. Last thing he wanted was to lead the gunmen to Alyssa and Thomas, so instead of bearing left to the clinic rooms, he turned right to the admin corridor with its empty offices.

He took a moment to aim his light down the hall, making sure there were no major obstacles, but this area had already been stripped bare, even the light fixtures were gone, the corridor complete barren of everything except drywall and linoleum.

Light off, moving through the dark, he hadn't gone far when the sound of soft footfalls made him freeze. Behind him. Someone skilled enough that they'd come through the double doors silently.

He clutched his pistol tight as he slipped into an empty office, back pressed against the wall. The footsteps approached. Blake held his breath. The guy was good, but the smarter play would've been to use a light, not play pussy-foot. Maybe the guy didn't have the training to know how to use a tactical light without making himself a target? Maybe he enjoyed feeling like a predator, stalking his prey. If so, he was about to have the tables turned on him.

Suddenly, the intercom in the ceiling above came to life. "To the intruder…"

Blake's gut twisted with fury as the hostage taker finished his threat. But his pursuer, now just inches away, outside the door to the room where Blake hid, had another reaction. He whooped, leaping high to rattle the intercom speaker.

"Way to go, Mercer. Didn't think you had it in you, man." He continued down the hallway before Blake could jump him. But with that comment, condemning innocent civilians to a needless death, the man cemented his fate.

Blake was going to kill him.

He followed, tracking the man by sound alone.

A fine plan. Until Blake lost him. He backtracked and realized the man had turned down one of the short hallways that intersected with the abandoned section where Alyssa and Thomas were hiding.

Dammit. He needed to get ahead of the man, block his path to Alyssa and Thomas.

Blake slipped through a side door into the first office, as barren as the rest of the admin corridor, taking careful steps to avoid making any noise. His senses were on high alert, every misplaced footstep on the grimy floor was a potential threat to expose his position.

He slipped through the series of interconnected offices, ready to spring into action at any moment, pausing at each doorway, straining his ears for any sound of the gunman.

Then he ran out of offices, reaching the final

connecting corridor. He turned toward the clinic hallway. Alyssa and Thomas were only three rooms away.

A muffled cry sounded through the darkness.

Alyssa. His stomach dropped. He was too late.

Avoiding the debris he'd noted earlier, he closed in to the only room with light streaming out. Through the partially open door, he caught sight of the gunman, silhouetted by the Maglite's beam. The man loomed over Alyssa, who lay pale and still on the gurney. Thomas was nowhere to be seen.

Blake's grip tightened on his pistol. He took a deep breath, steadying himself. He had to act fast, but one wrong move could put Alyssa in even more danger.

He stepped forward toward the doorway, his foot skated slightly on a worn linoleum section, releasing a tiny squeak.

Shit.

The man turned away from Alyssa and looked directly at Blake. Perched on the top of his head were night vision goggles—one mystery answered.

But the most important thing, the thing Blake's mind, his entire body, was totally focused on, was that the man had the muzzle of his semiautomatic resting against Alyssa's temple.

"Join the party," he said in a tone that held both humor and threat. AKA psycho. Figured.

"Alright," Blake said steadily. "I'm coming in. Don't do anything stupid."

"Stay where I can see you and keep it slow. Otherwise, your friend will die to regret it." Psycho-guy grinned at his own joke, yet another tip off to his altered mental status.

Blake stepped into the doorway, hands raised, pistol dangling from his finger by the trigger guard.

"Drop the piece," Psycho ordered.

Blake complied, crouching to set it to the floor, then standing once more. Last thing they needed was for a misfire.

"Hands in the air."

"You guys already shot her once, you really gonna shoot her again? Why don't you try a new target, someone more challenging than a girl," Blake said, his tone laced with contempt.

"Just buying leverage, asshole. Now get on your knees, slowly. Then we'll see how you feel about playing target."

Blake eased himself onto his knees, which was an effort with his hands up. Not to mention his old injury made his leg stiff especially in the cold weather. The blade inside his boot twisted slightly. He'd almost forgotten about it.

Psycho moved toward him, eyes wide, pupils dilated with more than just adrenaline. Christ, the guy was high on something. Erratic, irrational, irritable, this guy had it all going on.

Before Blake could deliver a PSA on the dangers of mixing guns and drugs, Psycho flipped his pistol around and whacked Blake across the side of the head. Blake crumpled lower to the floor, bracing himself with a palm while his other hand went to his head and felt sticky, warm blood oozing there. His vision swam for a moment and nausea clenched his gut, but a few deep breaths cleared his head.

Psycho moved around him as if eying a particularly interesting specimen. Blake moved his hand slowly from his skull to his ankle, pretending his balance was wobbly after the blow, his fingers brushing the knife handle inside his boot.

"Hands back up!"

Blake grimaced and raised his hands.

"Please," Alyssa said. "Please don't—"

"It's okay, Alyssa, it's okay," Blake said calmly.

"Ya think? Well, we'll see about that." Psycho rammed a knee into his back. Blake flowed with the blow, acting as if it had made him buckle, one palm slapping the floor, the other slipping his knife free.

With a practiced motion, he thumbed the blade open and stabbed the man's popliteal fossa, twisting the blade behind and under the kneecap to do as much damage as possible before yanking it free.

Psycho let out a yelp, aiming his pistol at…where Blake had been before he slammed his entire weight into a tackle, driving Psycho back, out of the room, away from Alyssa.

They crashed into the wall opposite the door.

Blake's hands locked onto Psycho's pistol arm, wrestling for control of the weapon.

Tangled together, they hit the floor hard, Psycho's head cracking against the linoleum. Blake used the other man's momentary daze to his advantage, twisting his wrist with all his strength. The gun clattered to the ground, skittering across the floor.

Psycho thrashed beneath him, trying to jab Blake with his elbow. But Blake still held his knife, and he knew how to use it. He didn't just plunge the blade into Psycho's thigh, he targeted the area around the femoral blood vessels with repeated punching stabs. All he needed was for one to hit the vein—a more deadly wound than an arterial blow, but Blake would be happy with either.

Blood streamed freely from Psycho's thigh as Blake pinioned the man, straddling his chest to keep him down. All Blake had to do was hold this position, and the wounds would do the rest. He'd bleed out, and it would be over.

Maybe it was the drugs in his system, but somehow Psycho found the strength to send his hips flying up, bucking Blake off. Then he spun around, slamming his elbow into Blake's exposed back.

Blake grunted as pain shot up his spine. He fought to maintain his position, knowing he couldn't let Psycho gain the upper hand. He used the wall for leverage—and to protect his back from another blow, climbing upright just as Psycho came at him, fingers outstretched like claws. The blood had soaked the man's pants, puddling on the floor, but Psycho wouldn't give up, lips curled into a rictus grin, showing his teeth as he lunged and tried to dig his fingers into Blake's eyeballs.

Blake blocked the frenzied attack, and Psycho laughed. The kind of laugh that would haunt Blake's nightmares for a long time, he was sure. Blake spotted a stray wheelchair tipped sideways, gave it a hard shove, and used it to flip Psycho backwards onto the floor. The damn fool somehow rolled over and tried to crawl away, but Blake easily caught him once more.

"Just...stay...down," Blake growled through gritted teeth, pressing his total weight onto Psycho's chest.

The man's eyes were wide with panic, and his breath came in ragged gasps.

Blake watched the fight draining from the man, replaced by the sudden realization he was dying. For a moment, Blake was transported back to that goddamn highway in Afghanistan, watching the light fade from Miller's eyes as they stared into Blake's soul.

Blake kept his grip firm, watching as consciousness slowly slipped away from the man beneath him. When Psycho's body finally went limp, Blake cautiously released his hold.

He checked for a pulse, finding none.

It was over.

Blake pushed himself to his feet, breathing heavily,

wincing at the pain in his back. He stumbled over to where the gunman's pistol had fallen, scooping it up and checking the magazine. Half full.

Better than nothing. He trudged back to Alyssa.

"Blake," Alyssa whispered weakly, her voice barely audible.

"Yeah, still here." He checked her vitals—oxygen too low, pulse too high, despite her needle decompression. Jeezit, no way in hell he'd ever have the guts to do that to himself. "Shit, Alyssa. You're one tough bi—"

"Boss," she finished for him. She gestured to the O2 tank, and he realized that was part of the problem. Easy enough fix. With well-practiced moves, he grabbed one of the spare tanks and the wrench and had her switched over in a matter of seconds. The pulse ox began to climb up, although still was nowhere near where he'd like it.

"Where's Thomas?"

She moved her head slightly from side to side. "Don't…know. Left."

Blake cursed under his breath. The last thing he needed was Thomas getting himself into trouble. Where could he have gone? The old man couldn't see enough to make it out the construction exit much less drive anywhere. Which meant….

No. Oh, no.

Blake glanced at his watch. The five minutes weren't up yet. He was pretty sure the hostage takers wouldn't kill their only bargaining chips, but after meeting Psycho…. And if Thomas heard the announcement…

Shit. Shit, shit, shit.

He grabbed his pistol from the floor. It had a full mag, so he gave Alyssa Psycho's weapon. "Just in case," he told her.

"Get Thomas."

"Aim to."

He had a plan. Well, half of a plan. But he had to go big if he was going to provide enough of a diversion to pull the gunmen away from the hostages and Thomas. If only Thomas didn't get himself killed before Blake could reach him.

He grabbed the eight-ounce bottles of hand sanitizer from both the trauma bag and the med kit. "I'll be back," he told Alyssa.

It only took a few seconds to position Psycho in the wheelchair. Thankfully, the wheels worked fine even if the leather seat was torn. Blake sped the dead man down the hall toward the ER, dousing Psycho in the alcohol-based sanitizing solution as they went.

He paused at the double doors, tucking his pistol in his belt—his drill sergeant would have howled at that—and slipping his knife back in its sheath. Then he dug his old Zippo from his inside jacket pocket. Blake didn't smoke. It was a good luck charm he always carried with him, had seen his grandfather through Vietnam.

And now it was about to save a bunch of innocent civilian's lives.

If Blake could pull this off.

Chapter Twenty-Four

FRIDAY, February 13th, 9:26 P.M.

SARA SAT WITH CONNOR, doing what she could to make him comfortable but keep him lucid enough to convince his brother not to kill everyone. The nitrous had run out, so she switched him back to a non-rebreather mask. He said he wasn't in pain, didn't want her to give him any sedation—she could have used the lorazepam in the crash cart, kept there for seizures—so she was reduced to sitting beside him, holding his hand.

She'd just turned the monitor alarms off—his heart rate alarm kept blaring—when the intercom sounded with Mercer's voice. Sara listened to his threat, her own heart rate speeding much too fast.

"Five minutes. Starting now," Mercer finished.

"He can't—he wouldn't—" she said.

"He would," Connor said with a sigh.

She whirled on him. "How do I stop him?"

His face contorted with emotion. "Andrew's obsessed with the rubies."

"Rubies? Are those what you stole? Are innocent people dying because of some damned rubies?" Her voice rose, and Connor flinched.

Dying man and her patient. She forced herself calm, resuming her seat beside him.

"The Bitterroot Stars. They're everything to him. But they're cursed. They'll destroy him," Connor whispered. "Take them." He gestured with the finger his pulse ox was on, pointing to Luca's body and his own bloody clothes they'd cut him out of. "They're in my shirt pocket."

"What good will they do me?" she asked, then answered her own question. "Hostages. I run with the rubies, offer to exchange them for the hostage's safety." It meant sacrificing her own life. Mercer would never let her live, not after that, she was certain.

But Mercer was ready to kill everyone anyway. Die now, save lives; die later, lose lives.

Easy equation.

Sara moved over to the pile of bloody clothing, forcing herself to ignore Luca's body. But it wasn't Luca, not anymore. Just a lump of cold, bloody flesh.

She dragged out everything Connor had been wearing. His shirt was in shreds but the pockets were intact—and empty. As were the cargo pants pockets—all of them, even the tiny, hidden one inside the front pocket. She checked his boots, the pouches that lined his ballistic vest, his jacket.

She turned back to him. "Nothing. They're not here."

HANDS on the wheelchair's handles, Blake stood outside the double doors separating the unused wing from the ER wing. He had two options for approaching the waiting room where the hostages and gunmen were: turn right and take the fastest approach directly to the main doors, or turn left and go through the triage area, which would provide him more cover and increase the element of surprise. The only drawback was that maneuvering the wheelchair through two sets of doors would cost him a few seconds, but he decided it'd be worth it.

The intercom came to life once more. "Time's up. I'm gonna start shooting. A hostage every five minutes. Their blood is on your hands."

Blake gripped his Zippo, the man's words igniting his blood as if it was him on fire. He opened the door, ready to plow through it, safety be damned, when he saw a man walking toward the waiting room from the direction of the nurse's station. He wore tactical gear like the others, rifle slung to his back, pistol in his hand. From the set of his jaw, this had to be the leader.

He watched through the doors as the man approached two men standing at the main entrance leading into the waiting room. They were close enough he could hear them once he cracked the door open.

"Who's it gonna be, Mercer?" one of the guards asked the leader.

Mercer. Blake wasn't going to forget that name.

Since he'd taken down two men already, and someone had to be injured given the blood in the EMS bay, these three must be the only ones left. And they were all here, together, the perfect target.

If it wasn't for the oblique angle and two civilians potentially in the line of fire, he might have considered going for a shot. But even if he downed one of them, the other two held weapons, could unleash a barrage on the hostages.

No. Best to stick with his plan.

While the men were focused on the hostages, he opened the doors and wheeled his alcohol-soaked package through, turning toward the triage area. He typed in his key code and entered the small hall behind the triage assessment cubicles. From here, he had a good view into the waiting room, could plan his trajectory.

The hostages sat in chairs lined up against the far wall, across from Blake. Their hands were bound in front of them with duct tape, but their legs seemed free of restraints. Good, they'd be able to run for it once he caught the gunmen's attention.

Mercer entered the room, standing in the middle, facing the hostages, which put him and his men's backs to Blake. Mercer aimed his pistol in a sweeping motion across the faces of the terrified hostages, landing on a young boy wearing a hockey shirt.

Blake began his countdown.

One… He flipped the Zippo open.

In two quick strides, Mercer reached the child and yanked him up by the arm. The boy's mother jumped up to protect him, her voice piercing the tense silence. "No! Please, not my son! Please!"

Two…Blake lined the wheelchair up on a diagonal that would carry it across the linoleum directly at Mercer and his men. His finger hovered over the Zippo's striker.

"Shut up," Mercer told her. One of his men—Harper, the man Blake had fought with earlier—stepped forward to force her back into her seat.

Behind the wheelchair, Blake crouched low, ready to push off. Harper stepped away from the woman. Perfect…

Blake struck the Zippo, the lighter flaming into life.

Mercer yanked the kid's head back, pistol pressed to his temple. Tears tracked down the boy's face.

Pure terror.

Blake shoved the wheelchair as hard as he could and—

Three! Blake tossed the lighter into Psycho's lap.

"Stop that," came a commanding voice from the waiting room door.

Thomas! Shit, the old man had bad timing. But it was too late for Blake to do anything except draw his gun and pray for a clear shot before Thomas got himself killed.

Mercer and his men spun to face the new threat even as Psycho's body whooshed into a fiery, ballistic missile racing toward their blindside.

Blake raised his pistol, finger on the trigger, ready to fire. Thomas, god bless him, had stumbled forward, now stood directly in Blake's line of fire, blocking his shot.

Fire alarms blared to life, crescendoing, filling the room with a chaotic cacophony.

Hostages screamed, the sound jagged, as they flung themselves away from the wheelchair careening into the room.

Mercer, blind panic etching his face, let loose of the boy. He and his men whirled to unleash a firestorm at the flaming figure in the wheelchair.

A series of metallic clicks sounded from above. A rush of water sheeted down.

Blake fought to get a clear shot, but Thomas, confused by the noise, the water no doubt adding to his disorientation, kept moving between him and his targets. Blake had no choice but to leave cover, enter the open space of the waiting area.

The gambit paid off. Finally, he had a shot at Mercer.

As he raised his pistol, a stray bullet hit his arm. Adrenaline blocked any real pain, but the impact threw his aim off, his shots thudding into the wall beside the door, missing their target.

The wheelchair finally came to a halt, the body slumped to the side, riddled with bullets.

The sharp smell of gunpowder and a sickening stench of burning flesh filled the air, burning Blake's throat, and bent him over, coughing.

He looked up as the second gunman, a squat guy with a mohawk, moved through the smoke, brandishing a fire extinguisher in his meaty hands. White foam sprayed, covering the burning figure in the wheelchair, adding to the sprinkler dousing. The air grew thick with a choking fog.

Blake's visibility dropped to near zero, his world becoming a swirling, opaque nightmare as he lost sight of Thomas and one of the gunmen, Harper, in the confusion. He ignored his wounded arm, dripping blood inside his coat sleeve, as he tried to isolate his targets, but acrid smoke stung his eyes, making it impossible to see clearly. The backdrop of screams from the hostages blurred into the moment's soundtrack.

He heard Mercer's voice: "Take this, you fuck!" followed by a sickening thud and a pained groan from Thomas.

Blake's stomach twisted. As the smoke cleared, Blake caught a glimpse of Mercer shoving Thomas against the wall. His every instinct demanded that he surge forward to protect the old man, but his tactical training took over. As soon as the smoke cleared, he'd be exposed, without cover, totally vulnerable. He had no choice but to run.

Even worse, he'd achieved total mission failure.

All three gunmen were unharmed, and now Thomas was the new target of their fury.

Chapter Twenty-Five

FRIDAY, February 13th, 9:36 P.M.

WAVING AWAY THE DISSIPATING SMOKE, Brick assessed the situation. Harper was nowhere to be seen, but the hostages were all present, including the new one, the old man. No way this geezer was the intruder who'd beat the shit out of Harper.

He looked down at the smoldering, charred corpse in the wheelchair. Leon—he recognized the gold chains. Smoke still curled from the ruined body, a sight that turned his stomach and ignited a fire in his chest. Leon. Brick had been sure that mo'fucker was indestructible.

A knot of rage threatened to throttle him. Leon's death wasn't on that intruder or any of the others. No, this fell squarely on Mercer.

He whirled on Mercer, grabbed him by the shoulder, and hauled him to the hallway outside the waiting room. The sprinklers weren't going out here. The smoke was thin, although the stench was still pungent, at least he could breathe.

He leaned forward to shout over the alarms, "We need to go. Grab the rubies and let's go. Now."

If Mercer had focused on their goal—the jewels—none of this would've happened. They wouldn't be holed up in this shithole of a clinic, waiting for the inevitable swarm of cops to descend. What was the escape plan exactly? Brick was no Einstein, but he could see a shitshow when it flung crap at his face like some nasty pie fight.

Mercer stood his ground, shrugging Brick's hands off him. He raised his pistol between them, could've blown Brick's face off if he pulled the trigger.

Brick stepped back. Mercer lowered his weapon.

"Not. Without. My. Brother." Mercer gritted the words out. Then he spun on his heel and strode down the hall to the room where Connor was busy dying. If he wasn't dead already.

Brick glanced back into the waiting room. The hostages had clumped together as far away from the smoldering wheelchair as possible, crying and coughing and freaking out. Except the old man, who was on the floor against the wall beside the door where Mercer had thrown him.

Brick wouldn't hesitate to kill them all in an instant if it meant getting those rubies for himself and getting outta here. But right now, that would achieve zero.

Only Mercer knew where the rubies were.

Mercer.

His fists clenched at his sides as he took one last look at Leon's charred remains. The rubies were supposed to be their ticket out, but they'd become a curse, just like that Watts guy had said.

He turned and moved down the corridor, pulling a

hunting knife from his belt just as the distant sound of sirens whispered on the wind.

~

MERCER STORMED into the operating room, eyes blazing with such fury that Sara turned to place herself between him and her patient.

"Hey! Where'd the nurses go? You let them go?" He moved toward her menacingly.

She stood her ground, meeting his gaze with a steady calm she didn't feel. "You promised to let them leave once Connor stabilized. He's awake and talking."

Mercer stuttered to a stop, his gaze raking over the gurney with its clean sheet, blood free. Sara held her breath as he approached Connor, taking the seat she'd vacated.

Connor turned his head toward his brother. "Andrew, listen. You gotta get out of here, before it's too late. Just go —live your life. This all isn't worth dying for."

Mercer gripped the edge of the gurney and smiled at his brother, ignoring his words. "Hey, Connor. How you doing? Listen, we're both getting outta here, okay? Nothing's changed. We're in this together, remember?"

"Not anymore." Connor's voice was barely above a whisper. "It's over, Andrew. Let it go. I'm not gonna make it."

For a moment, Sara thought she saw a flicker of doubt in Mercer's eyes, a softening of his resolve.

Then he leaned over Connor, their faces close together. "I'm sorry I let you down, bro. I fucked up, big time."

Connor stared at Mercer for a long moment. "It's okay. I love you, Andrew. Forget the rubies, go live your life. For me."

Mercer embraced his brother. Sara was finally able to take a full breath again. It was over. Connor had gotten through to him, thank god. Mercer would take his men and leave her people alive.

"Mercer!" Brick appeared in the doorway, knife in hand, face in shadow, eyes blazing with hate.

~

BLAKE, clutching his arm in his blood-soaked jacket, hid behind a triage desk, watching Brick stalk away. He had not seen that coming. And still no sign of the other gunman, Harper.

Blake rushed to Thomas first. The old man smiled up at him weakly. "Did we get them?"

"Yeah, Thomas. We whupped them good. Ready to blow this pizza joint?"

Thomas nodded.

Blake helped him up, turned to the other hostages. A few were already freeing each other from their restraints.

"Follow me," he told them, handing his knife to the man who'd come in with the lady with the broken arm. "I work here, I know the way out. We should hurry, I don't know when they'll be back."

The patients moved slowly, unsure. Everyone was holding someone else as if unwilling to venture out alone. And none of them would meet Blake's eyes. Did they think he was one of the bad guys?

Thomas waved for their attention. "This is Blake, he's a medic. Saved my life more times than I can count. Come with us if you want to live."

The kid in the hockey jersey gave a nervous laugh at Thomas's horrible Terminator impression.

His mom grabbed his hand, strode over to Blake. "Let's

go, people." Her voice was that of a woman used to corralling young boys. Command presence, they called it in the Army. "Everyone got their hands free? Okay, no one alone, get a partner and follow us." She lasered her gaze at the ward clerk, Angie. "You're in charge of making sure no one gets left behind."

With that, she nodded to Blake, and he draped an arm around Thomas, leading them out to freedom. When they turned into the dark corridor leading to where Alyssa was, a few protested, but Hockey Mom kept them herded in the right direction, no stragglers. Blake wouldn't have minded having a few of her with him on patrol back in the shitstorm.

He was glad for the lack of lighting hiding Psycho's blood spattered over the walls and pooled on the floor. It was too cold to have them wait outside into a blizzard, so he sent the kid and his mom to gather chairs so they could sit in the more defensible corridor that connected to the office wing. Just in case.

"The police might come in the rear doors." He pointed down Alyssa's hallway to the exit. "Just keep still, hold your hands up, and stay quiet. Follow their commands."

With the hostages taken care of, he led Thomas into Alyssa's room where he could check him out properly. Poor guy was going to have a black eye and his nose looked broken, but his sugar was doing okay.

"Potassium's higher," he told Alyssa. She'd taken one look at Thomas and waved Blake away from her to evaluate the old man first.

"Needs dialysis," she told Blake. "Soon."

Her color was worse, he noted.

"I'm fine," Thomas protested. "Blake, take care of Alyssa. She needs you more than I do."

He reached for the stethoscope, but Alyssa batted him away.

"Hemo-pneumo," she gasped. Shit. "Nothing. You. Can. Do."

Except pray the cops got here fast and brought ALS medics with them. Unless…Sara. She'd be able to help.

He'd saved everyone else. Except the one person he'd come here to save.

As usual, Alyssa followed his thoughts. "Sara," she said. "Get. Sara."

"On it, boss."

Chapter Twenty-Six

FRIDAY, February 13th, 9:41 P.M.

MERCER RELEASED Connor and turned to face Brick. His old cellmate held his Glock in one hand, but it was the other hand, the one gripping a nasty-looking hunting knife, that got Mercer's attention. Brick had a reputation for enjoying carving on people, convincing them to tell him what he wanted to know.

Mercer never thought Brick would dream of using the blade on him. But that was the problem with making friends with fellow inmates. You couldn't trust any of them.

He didn't waste time on small talk or bargaining. Instead, he fired his own semiautomatic. It was a quick shot, almost without aiming, so he was gratified to see he'd hit the meaty part of Brick's gun arm.

Brick shouted in pain, dropping his pistol.

Mercer tried to fire again, but this time his weapon jammed. He cried out in frustration, tossing the pistol aside.

Fueled with rage, he lunged across the room at Brick, who crouched on the floor, scrambling to grab his Glock. Mercer had come too far, sacrificed too much, to let this backstabbing traitor destroy everything.

Brick slashed wildly with his knife, but Mercer's instincts were already kicking in, honed by years of street fights and prison brawls. He dodged the blade, feeling it whistle past his ear.

Then he grabbed Brick's wrist, dug his fingers into the flesh, and twisted hard. There was a satisfying crack, followed by Brick's muffled grunt of pain, and the knife clattered to the floor.

But Brick wasn't done.

Before Mercer could press his advantage, Brick's forehead smashed into Mercer's face with brute force. The impact sent Mercer staggering back, his vision blurring as pain exploded through him and a familiar taste of copper filled his mouth. Warm blood gushed from his now-broken nose, and for a moment, his world spun fast, but he forced himself to focus. He'd endured worse in prison and survived beatings that would have killed a lesser man. Brick may have landed a good hit, but Mercer was far from finished. He wouldn't let a little pain stop him, not when he was so close to everything he'd fought for.

Mercer tackled Brick, driving the other man into the wall, using all his weight. Medical equipment crashed to the floor around them as they grappled. With a roar of fury, Mercer slammed his knee into Brick's groin. As Brick doubled over, Mercer grabbed him by his mohawk and smashed his face into his rising knee.

Once, twice, three times.

Mercer let Brick crumple to the floor, then stomped on Brick's hand. Bones crunched under Mercer's boot, and he reached for the fallen knife, then snatched up Brick's pistol, aiming at the back of the motionless, seemingly uncon-scious man's head.

"Andrew!"

Mercer stopped at his brother's voice and returned to Connor, breathing heavily from the exertion of the fight. The doctor stepped aside and hit a button that silenced the stupid beeping machine.

"Hey, bro. Sorry about all the commotion, but Brick here just tried to stab us in the back." He grinned through blood-soaked teeth. "Didn't work out for him, though."

"Andrew," Connor repeated through hoarse gasps. "Leave. Now. Before the cops get here."

Mercer frowned at his brother. After all this, did Connor seriously think he'd give up on him?

But then he heard the sound of sirens. Fuckin' hell.

"Time's up." Connor's words were barely audible. Didn't matter. They still shook Mercer to the core.

BLAKE CREPT along the hall toward the trauma bay, where the grunts and animalistic noises of two men beating the shit out of each other echoed toward him, along with a series of urgent beeps from a monitor. Someone was having a very bad day, that rapid bleeping told him.

Pistol at the ready, he edged to the doorway, sidling to an angle where he could appraise the situation. The men had gone quiet, and when he looked, he saw Mercer standing over a younger guy who lay on a gurney. Mohawk lay on the ground, motionless, while Sara stood by an instrument cart, staring at Blake as if he'd come bearing roses.

Not that, battered and bruised as he was, Blake was in any fit state for a date night. Still, seeing that smile aimed solely at him, gave him a thrill more powerful than any amount of adrenaline could.

Mercer, sensing a change in Sara, whirled. He met Blake's gaze, even as he raised his weapon with one hand, wrapping his other around Sara, gathering her as a shield in front of him. He positioned his pistol at her chest, directly above her heart.

"Drop it, now!" Mercer ordered.

Blake's combat-honed instincts screamed at him to take the head shot, but he couldn't risk missing. He lowered his gun to his side.

"Mercer, it's over." Blake uttered the words with complete calm, hoping to reason or at least distract as he slowly eased forward to close the space, stepping over Brick's out-flung arm. "I don't give a shit about you or what you did to end up here. Just leave. Go. Now."

A flicker of indecision crossed Mercer's face. For a split second, Blake thought he might have gotten through. But then Mercer's gaze flicked down to Brick's body on the floor beside Blake.

Brick lunged, grabbing both Blake's heels. His world tilted as his feet pulled out from under him. He crashed to the floor, his gun skittering away. Pain exploded through his shoulder as he hit the linoleum hard. He rolled, narrowly avoiding Brick's follow-up stomp as the other man jumped up, surprisingly agile given that his face was a bloody pulp.

Blake scrambled to his feet, his body screaming in protest. He dove for his gun, fingers closing around the grip just as Brick's fist connected with his jaw. Stars exploded across his vision. As they grappled, Mercer stepped away from the gurney, circling the two men, trying to get a clear shot.

Blake caught a flash of movement from Sara, still

behind Mercer. She held something sharp and shiny, then struck with lightning precision, driving a metal trocar deep into Mercer's ear.

Mercer's gun discharged, the report deafening in the confined space just as Blake pushed Brick away from him. For a terrifying moment, Blake thought he'd been hit. But it was Brick who stumbled back, clutching his shoulder, blood seeping between his fingers.

Taking advantage of the opening Brick had given him, Blake lunged at him, crashing them into a supply cart, sending surgical instruments clattering to the floor. Blake ended on top of the other man. He circled his arm around Brick's throat, leveraged his other arm against it, choking the man until he slumped in Blake's arms. He could have eased up then, but no way in hell was he about to allow an enemy alive behind him and he needed to ensure Sara's safety.

Blake finished Brick for good. Then stood.

Chaos surrounded him.

Sara was backing away from Mercer, who had dropped his gun to raise his hand to his ear, turning to face her.

Connor's pale face as his eyes drifted shut.

The vital signs on the monitor flatlining.

But Blake couldn't focus on anything beyond the immediate threat. "Sara!"

Blake lunged toward Mercer, whose eyes were almost popping out of his skull in a look of complete shock as he staggered toward Sara, his hand clutching at the trocar sticking out from his ear, blood spraying down to his shoulder.

Blake grabbed the handle of the device, an eight-inch steel instrument used for invasive surgery, and wrenched it out. Mercer howled, the blood-curdling scream of an animal.

With the sharp metal device clutched in his hand, Blake stabbed it hard, right into Mercer's chest, angling to slide over his ribs and directly into his heart.

Mercer staggered back. His wide eyes dropped to the alien tool protruding out of his chest. A shaking hand reached up for it and weakly grasped the handle. He opened his mouth as if to say something, but one side of his face seemed to freeze.

"Probably not a good idea," Blake warned.

Then, in a whisper, Mercer managed to speak. "The stars are…cursed."

He slumped down onto his knees, his mouth falling open as he keeled over onto his hands and knees, dribbling blood, droplets splattering onto the floor. Then he collapsed, all his strength gone, and lay like a curled-up fetus, spasming, before the movement stopped, his eyes staring at Blake, the man who'd killed him.

Chapter Twenty-Seven

FRIDAY, February 13th, 11:11 P.M.

THE OLD CLINIC wing had transformed into a hive of swarming medical personnel, first responders, and State Police officers.

The hostages, wrapped in emergency foil blankets, sipped hot drinks while being checked over by Sara and fussing Potsdam medics while waiting their turn to be interviewed by the State Police. Sara had refused to talk to the police until she finished treating all her patients and saw her staff safe, so Blake had gone first. It had taken the better part of an hour to walk the staties through everything.

Now, the aftermath of the adrenaline crash had left him too tired to do more than sit and watch Sara work her magic.

Alyssa left on the first ambulance. Sara had insisted, Thomas told Blake, explaining that she'd need a full trauma eval and a chest tube.

Sara wanted Thomas to go in the same ambulance, but he'd absconded—his word—only to be returned by police officers. Twice. Until Sara finally relented, deciding if he was stable enough to wander around a crime scene, he was stable enough to wait. On the caveat that he stay close to a medical provider and let them monitor him.

The smirk on Thomas's face was wider than a Cheshire cat's as he caught Blake up with everything that had happened while Blake was with the troopers and getting the wound to his arm treated. Luckily the bullet had only grazed him.

"Most excitement I had in decades," Thomas told Blake. "No way in hell was I gonna leave early and miss anything."

They sat on a pair of chairs in the hallway where Blake had parked the hostages, who were now leaving two by two. Blake had never seen Sara like this, triaging multiple patients while simultaneously providing comfort. The Potsdam medics followed after her, making notes, cleaning wounds, applying dressings, guiding patients to the chaplain trained in trauma counseling who Sara had called in.

"They made a lethal mistake," Thomas said as he nibbled on M&M's—plain, not peanut, the nuts messed with his partials—from the bag Blake had busted open the vending machine to get him. At least the cops had brought in portable heaters and turned the lights on, so they weren't sitting in the dark. "The crooks, I mean."

He waited for Blake to take the bait. Blake resisted, but only for a few moments. How could anyone resist Thomas? Besides, the old man was a hero, deserved a bit of indulgence.

"What was their lethal mistake?" Blake asked.

"They mistook me for a frail, helpless, blind man."

"Don't forget old."

"Okay. Frail, helpless, old blind man. But," he wiggled a finger in admonishment, "that was all part of my master plan. Fooled them, didn't I?"

"Walking into my line of fire and almost getting yourself shot was part of the plan?" The words came out a bit sharper than Blake wanted. He was still angry at Thomas for putting himself in danger.

The old man clasped Blake's arm. "No, that's part of being blind. The biggest part of my plan was you, Blake. I had absolute faith that you were there, somewhere, ready to save the day. And you did."

Blake inhaled sharply. He'd almost gotten them all killed. Almost gotten Sara killed. "I'm no hero. I'm just glad it worked out, and we're all alive."

"And that, my boy, is my point. We are all alive. Including the most amazing woman you'll ever be lucky enough to meet in this lifetime. Just like my Rose. But you need to let her know how you feel—luck doesn't come around twice."

Sara's murmurs reached them from down the hall. She was sharing her feelings, inviting Evan and his mom to do the same, trying to get them started on the path to healing. It was a profoundly personal thing to witness. Blake felt a strange combination of awe, anxiety, and…anger.

He wasn't even remotely worthy of her, much less ready to give her a glimpse of his true self, a wounded warrior that had to fight each day just to open his eyes and keep on breathing.

Plus, he was finally getting better with his routine, his structure, his carefully crafted environment. Was he really going to risk all that? What if he did and she didn't feel the same? Could his perfectly balanced life survive that?

His pulse raced and his throat tightened, unable to allow any air into his lungs. Christ, just the thought of the pain of her rejection…and he was having a full-blown panic attack.

"Breathe," Thomas whispered, his grip tightening on Blake's arm, providing an anchor to reality. "In. One, two, three, four. Hold. Out. One, two, three, four."

Blake's body followed the old man's command, and suddenly, Blake was in control again. But it only proved how easily he could lose it. He couldn't ask anyone to share a life like his.

"Take advice from an old, weathered fool," Thomas interrupted Blake's racing spiral of doom. "Life won't wait for us idiot humans to somehow achieve perfection. You gotta embrace the good and bad, warts and all. Hitch your pants up and find the courage to grab what life sets in your path, kid." He held up his hand, the one with his wedding ring, and gave it a kiss. "Trust me. I should know."

Blake sighed, watching as the troopers escorted the last of the patients out, leaving Sara alone. She slipped into the empty exam room where he'd stashed Alyssa and Thomas earlier.

Kelly, the nurse, came in from the ambulance staging area, spotted Thomas. "There you are. Our ride's waiting. Time to go, Thomas."

Blake stifled his laugh as Thomas immediately appeared frail and doddering, letting Kelly help him up, leaning on her as he shuffled away. "Now then," he said, "tell me all about this fiancé of yours. Not sure he's good enough for a pretty girl like you, Miss Kelly."

They exited, and then it was just Blake and Sara.

How the hell did a walk of twenty feet down an empty hall take more courage than driving an RG-31 down the Highway to Hell?

Yet, somehow, he made it.

~

He found Sara, shoulders slumped, wielding a red biohazard trash bag, disposing of the bloody dressings and sheets left from Alyssa and Thomas. He approached her from behind, taking the bag from her, his other hand lying gently on her shoulder—an invitation. She slumped against him, still facing away. He understood that. Some things were best shared without eye contact.

"I killed him. He knew it, too. Knew exactly what I was doing, what I did…" She stripped the gloves from her hands, balled them up, let them fall to the floor. "He wasn't a bad kid. He even apologized, said he was sorry…" A choked sob reverberated through her. "And then, then…he thanked me."

Her entire body shuddered as she finally set her tears free. He turned her to him, let her bury her face in his chest and simply held her tight. There were times when human touch was the most powerful medicine in the world. Sara had taught him that.

Once she stopped crying, he still held her.

"I wish I had the words," he began. "But I'm not sure there are any." He took a deep breath, pulled her even closer. "They told me time would make things better. And it did, kinda, but it also dulled me. Made me oblivious. Living each day exactly like the last, like the next. I thought I was in control."

She tilted her head up to meet his gaze. It took everything he had not to flinch. "Two control freaks like you and me," she whispered. "When are we gonna learn, chaos always wins? It's a basic law of thermodynamics, entropy. The entire universe is hard-wired for self-destruction."

"Just like us humans." He shook his head and chuckled, surprising himself. "No. Not like us humans. We get to choose. Free will, remember? Those men, they chose. And suffered the consequences. You and I, we chose to put ourselves on the line to protect our patients, our friends. Yeah, there's a price to pay."

"There's always a price to pay," she agreed, but her tone was bitter.

"No. I mean, the price is worth it, right? Think of the lives we saved—you saved. They could've all died if you hadn't—"

She pushed away from him. "I understand what you're saying, but I should be saving lives, not taking them," she whispered, her voice wavering as she stared at the aftermath. "Men died tonight because of me."

"I know, I know." He wished she was back in his arms, but understood she needed space. "Like I was saying, time helps. A little. But you know what really made the difference, at least for me?"

She tore her gaze away from the blood on the floor beside her shoes, hauled in a deep breath, blew it out, and finally, finally looked up to meet his eyes once more. "Peanut M&M's?"

"Well, yeah, of course. But also friends to share them with. Friends to share everything with—the good and the bad."

A sheriff's deputy poked her head in the door. "Folks, we're securing this area, so you'll need to leave. Dr. Porter, the detectives are ready for your statement, if you'll come with me. Mr. Harrow, they said they have everything they need from you. You're free to go."

Sara's hand brushed his and he wrapped his fingers around hers. "You'll be fine, just walk them through everything, they don't bite." When the cops had finally arrived, he'd taken them through the events as thoroughly as if he'd been prepping an after-action report. "Maybe we could grab coffee after? I'll wait."

Sara squeezed his hand. "Thought you'd never ask. But none of that crap from the vending machines. If you want good coffee, we'll go to my place." She leaned into him and lowered her voice to a whisper. "I keep the best stuff there. How's tomorrow work for you?"

Tonight would be better, but they were both exhausted.

"Works for me." The needy, rough edge to his voice surprised him, but she actually turned and smiled as she left with the deputy.

Huh. All it took to get a date was a little murder and mayhem, go figure. Maybe for their second outing, he'd book time at a gun range.

Chapter Twenty-Eight

FRIDAY, February 13th, 11:58 P.M.

AFTER SARA LEFT, Blake felt the adrenaline seep from his body, leaving him physically and emotionally drained. He'd never felt so exhausted. The night of constant high adrenaline, high danger, and close combat had nearly wiped him out.

He headed out to the parking lot, hands in his jacket pockets. The snowstorm had passed, leaving only a light breeze scudding wispy clouds overhead. There were even a few stars visible. He gripped the handle of his truck door and yanked it open, but a nagging feeling tugged at the back of his mind.

Something wasn't right.

He closed the door again without getting in and scanned the area, his brow furrowed in concentration. The parking lot, dotted with haphazardly parked emergency vehicles and the remnants of the night's chaos, seemed eerily still.

He'd missed something. Something important.

Blake hurried back inside the building and straight to the trauma bay, standing outside the room where the bodies of Mercer and Brick lay in the same position that they had both died in. Connor's corpse was still on the cot, covered by a sheet. A forensic photographer circled the bodies, relentlessly snapping away and illuminating the room with bright flashes. The sterile smell of antiseptic mixed with the metallic tang of blood, creating an unsettling atmosphere.

Blake retraced his steps from there, arriving first at the nursing station where he'd unleashed the liquid nitrogen, freezing one thug's face, and brawled with the South African. Here, there were more forensic techs, swirling fingerprint brushes and wielding cameras. He saw the dead man's boots, but it hadn't been Blake's attack that killed him. It was the South African, Harper.

Where the hell was Harper? The cops had said there was no one to take into custody, only corpses. But Harper had been very much alive when Blake last saw him.

He waved to the CSI techs and continued down the hallway to the waiting room. Someone had covered Psycho's burnt body with a yellow plastic sheet and there was an officer standing guard at the door.

She looked up at him. "Sir, this is a restricted area. Do you have…"

"I'm looking for Dr. Porter? The detectives were interviewing her."

She nodded. "Right. They sent her home, were going to follow up with a formal interview tomorrow."

"She's gone?"

"I saw one of the SWAT officers escorting her out not two minutes ago."

Blake froze. "I don't think that was a police officer," he told her. "There's a gunman unaccounted for."

She frowned. "No, sir. I was told they accounted for all five hostage takers."

Blake had told the detectives everything he'd seen, but he hadn't actually sat down and counted how many gunmen he'd encountered.

He stopped, did a mental inventory: dead guy #1 at the nursing station, Psycho aka dead guy #2, mohawk guy, Mercer, Connor—also all dead.

Leaving Harper. "Not five. Six. Radio your supervisor. There's a man, South African accent, name of Harper— not sure if that's his first or last name. I think he impersonated a SWAT officer and escaped. Maybe with Dr. Porter."

She keyed her radio, but Blake wasn't about to stand around and wait. The cops had what they needed to start a search and send a car to Sara's home. No way in hell was he going to let her face potential danger alone. Not again.

He turned and ran, ignoring the officer's calls to wait. His heart pumped with terror as he burst through the main entrance doors and into the parking lot, his eyes frantically scanning the snow-covered ground.

As he approached the empty space where Sara's Subaru had been parked, Blake's gut twisted with dread. The imprint of her tires was still visible in the fresh snow, but something else caught his attention. Footprints. Men's boots. Alongside a woman's tracks. Leading from the staff exit to where Sara's car had been parked.

He spun to his truck, climbing in and jamming the key into the ignition before he even got the door shut.

"Please be wrong, please be wrong," he muttered as he gunned the engine, his truck lurching across to the exit.

A mass of tire tracks crisscrossed the white expanse— all the recent police and emergency services that had rolled into the hospital. But all tire tracks came and went in the direction of Potsdam, except one pair of tracks that headed off in the opposite direction toward Eastfork.

Blake scanned the road ahead, searching for any sign of Sara's car as he sped through the familiar landmarks of Eastfork. He lost the tracks when he hit the one section of town that had been plowed—the few blocks on either side of the fire department.

She said she was going home, and maybe that's just what she did—went home. Alone. But the nagging feeling in his gut wouldn't subside. He'd learned to trust his instincts in the war zone, and now they were screaming at him like a mad banshee.

Sara had hosted a staff BBQ last summer. It was the only time he'd been to her house, but he remembered she lived in a small development of mid-century ranches. He drove there, squinting to make out street signs and house numbers. All the houses appeared near-identical in the dark, their outlines blurred by the fallen snow.

"Maybe she's fine," he muttered, unable to convince himself. No sign of any cops, either.

Then he rounded a corner, a pair of red taillights flashing as they braked to pull into a driveway.

Blake's breath caught. Was it Sara's car?

Or was he chasing shadows, letting his paranoia get the best of him?

He slowed, switched off his lights, eased to a stop a few houses away. The vehicle ahead parked haphazardly. Definitely Sara's Subaru.

Two figures emerged from the car, barely visible in dark.

Blake held his breath as he recognized Sara's slender form being shoved toward the house by a taller, much broader figure. Harper, the South African. Had to be. He reached for his cell to call the cops but realized he didn't have it.

He watched the man push Sara through the front door, disappearing inside the darkened house. Blake's instincts screamed at him to rush in, to save Sara, but he forced himself to remain still. Rushing in mindlessly could put Sara in even more danger.

Blake quickly scanned the interior of his truck, his gaze settling on the glove compartment. He kept a long screwdriver in there. He snatched it up, testing the weight of the tool, and quietly opened the truck door. The snow crunched under his boots as he stepped out into the frigid night air, the screwdriver secured in his pocket.

The snow-covered yard offered little cover, but he kept low, his training kicking in as he assessed the situation. The house, like its neighbors, was a ranch with a detached garage. He shimmied up to a side window, peered into the dining room. The lights were on in the living room, and as he watched, more flicked on in the kitchen. He ducked low.

The kitchen was in the rear of the house, so he crept around to the front. Sara was smart. If she could, she would have left the door unlocked—she wouldn't want to limit her escape options. At least he prayed she'd been thinking clearly enough to do that.

He reached the front porch, made himself small as he approached the storm door, then opened it and reached to check the front door. Not only unlocked, but not quite latched. Smart lady.

Standing up just far enough to glance through the windows at the top of the door, he scanned the foyer and living room. No one.

He pushed the door open a crack and listened. Harper and Sara were still in the kitchen. Harper was demanding that Sara give him all her cash and access to her bank accounts. Sara was telling him her cash was hidden in her freezer. Stalling, Blake was sure, just as he was sure she had a plan.

Carefully, in case the hardwood floor creaked, he eased through the door and shut it before the cold could alert Harper. The foyer opened into the living room and the wall across from him had a brick fireplace. He spotted a poker beside it, hanging from a cast-iron base. The South African was bigger and stronger than Blake, and he'd moved as if he'd had some training—Blake had barely escaped him the first time they fought.

He switched his grip on the screwdriver and sidled across the open space to the fireplace. Blake eased the poker out from its stand and placed it on the hearth. Then he grasped the stand, feeling the solid weight of the iron in his hand. He tested its heft, gauging its potential as a weapon. It would do damage, more than the screwdriver or poker would, that much he knew.

He slid the screwdriver into his jacket pocket and planted himself against the wall, in Harper's blind spot when he emerged from the kitchen. The dark dining-room window he'd peered through earlier gave him a partial reflection of the kitchen. He couldn't see Harper, but he saw Sara, leaning into her freezer.

Now all he had to do was watch and wait.

But Sara had other ideas.

"Where's that cash?" Harper demanded.

"It's in here, but there's frost. I just need to dig it—"

She grabbed a bottle of vodka and swung it into the side of Harper's head, hard enough to stagger the man, sending him a step into the living room—

—right into Blake's path.

Blake wielded the heavy iron stand with all his might,

aiming it at the side of Harper's head. Before he could connect, Harper turned, the stand slamming into the man's neck and shoulder. The impact reverberated through Blake's arms, the force of the blow snapping his jaws together.

Harper merely gave a surprised grunt and spun around, crashing against the wall but somehow remaining upright. He raised his pistol and fired. The shot narrowly missed Blake, ripping past his ear, the bullet riding on a hot gust of air.

Blake swung again, this time aiming for Harper's gun arm, but Harper anticipated him, grabbing the poker stand with his other hand, yanking it from Blake, flinging it to the floor. Blake stumbled backward, Harper following with a kick to his belly that had Blake fighting for air. The room spun, his vision swimming from the impact.

Through watering eyes, Blake saw Harper regain his balance, a cruel smirk twisting his features. Time seemed to slow as the South African raised his weapon, the barrel pointing directly at Blake's chest.

A blur of movement caught his eye.

Sara appeared behind Harper. She gripped the iron poker stand, her knuckles white with the effort. She swung the heavy object, whacking the back of Harper's head with a nauseating thud. Harper's eyes rolled back before he crumpled to the ground like a puppet with its strings cut. His gun clattered to the floor, sliding across the hardwood and coming to rest at Blake's feet.

Sara stood over Harper's prone form, the poker stand still clutched in her trembling hands, chest heaving with rapid breaths.

Blake wasn't even sure she saw him. "Sara. Are you okay?"

"No. Not really," she managed to whisper in reply.

She stooped, carefully placed the blood-stained iron stand on the wooden floor, then slumped down onto her knees. "Oh, god, have I killed him?"

Blake got onto his knees and checked the man's pulse. "We're not that lucky. Got any duct tape?" He fished his own roll from his jacket, but it wouldn't be enough. He wanted this guy trussed tighter than a Thanksgiving turkey.

"Duct tape?" Her voice was distant as if translating from another language. Then her posture straightened, her focus returning with a snap. "I'm an ER doc, of course I have duct tape."

She stepped into the kitchen, opened a drawer, and tossed him a roll. It was neon pink. Of course it was. Actually made sense, here in the snow belt—if you needed it for an outdoor emergency, you wanted colors that were blazing bright, not dull gray that blended into the snow.

She returned with a Kershaw Onion knife that she opened with one hand.

"I like your taste in knives," he told her as she cut lengths of tape and he wrapped them around Harper's forearms and ankles.

"I like your timing." She rolled Harper onto his side into the recovery position. "Don't want him aspirating," she murmured.

Something hard fell out of Harper's pocket, rolling on the floor. Sara felt inside the pocket, emerged with four rubies in her palm. She held them out to Blake.

"Mercer said the 'stars are cursed.' Think those are what started all this?" Blake asked.

"That's what Connor told me. He said they were cursed as well." She dropped the gems as if they might bite her.

Then she turned to Blake. "How did you know?"

"Almost took me too long. I realized the cops had their

head count wrong—not surprising, given that no one left alive saw all of Mercer's gang together. Then I saw your car gone and one of the cops said you left with a SWAT guy and…" He shrugged. Then met her eyes. "But it was worth the trip. Someone told me you have the best coffee here?"

A wry smile curved Sara's lips. "I do." She sat back on her heels. The distant sound of a siren cut through the night. "Someone told me something, too. That it's better to spend time living than just live waiting for the right time."

"Thomas," he said. The old man just couldn't stop matchmaking, could he?

"Thomas," she confirmed.

"He's a very wise man." Blake scooted away from Harper. He placed an arm around Sara, drawing her in tight against him. "And always, always right."

She turned her face to his, and he met her halfway with a kiss that was much too short-lived, but plenty long enough to open an invitation for much, much more.

About the Authors

Nolon King writes fast-paced psychological thrillers set in the glitzy world of entertainment's power players with a bold, insightful voice. He's not afraid to explore the darker side of human nature through stories featuring families torn apart by secrets and lies.

Nolon loves to write about big questions and moral quandaries. How far would you go to cover up an honest mistake? Would you destroy your career to protect your family? How much of your soul would you sell to get the life of your dreams? Would you cheat on your husband to keep your children safe? Would you give in to a stalker's demands to save your marriage?

~

CJ Lyons *New York Times* and *USA Today* bestselling author of over forty novels, former pediatric ER doctor CJ Lyons has lived the life she writes about in her cutting-edge Thrillers with Heart.

CJ has been called a "master within the genre" (Pittsburgh Magazine) and her work has been praised as "breathtakingly fast-paced" and "riveting" (Publishers Weekly) with "characters with beating hearts and three dimensions" (Newsday).

She has assisted police and prosecutors with cases involving child abuse, rape, homicide and Munchausen by Proxy; and has worked in numerous trauma centers; as a crisis counselor; victim's advocate; as well as a flight physician for Life Flight. CJ credits her patients and their families for teaching her the art of medicine and giving her the courage to pursue her dream of becoming a novelist.

Her novels have twice won the International Thriller Writers' prestigious Thriller Award, the RT Reviewers' Choice Award, the Readers' Choice Award, the RT Seal of Excellence, and the Daphne du Maurier Award for Excellence in Mystery and Suspense. Also, CJ's short stories have appeared in anthologies edited by Lee Child and Margaret Atwood.

Over 3 million books sold worldwide.

Learn more about CJ's Thrillers with Heart at www.CJLyons.net

Also By Nolon King

The Nanny Problem

Rock-A-Bye-Bye

Nursery Crimes

Child's Prey

Replaced

Replaced

In Her Place

Irreplaceable

Cold Vengeance

Cold Vengeance

Cold Reckoning

Cold Retribution

Hidden Justice

Hidden Justice

Hidden Honor

Hidden Shame

Hidden Virtue

No Justice

No Justice

No Escape

No Hope

No Return

No Stopping

No Fear

Once Upon A Crime

Once Upon A Crime

Twice Upon A Lie

Three Times a Murder

Standalone Novels

Pretty Killer

12

Blown

Miserable Lies

The Target

Secrets We Keep

Close To Home

Heat To Obsession

A Simple Kill

Tell Me No Lies

Red Carpet Black

Fade To Black

Victim

Post Partum

www.ingramcontent.com/pod-product-compliance
Lightning Source LLC
Chambersburg PA
CBHW011118100726
47898CB00011B/3138